What Reader

David Marsh h
eulogy of the b
The beauty of his imagery in referring to God as the Maker "who speaks not in a voice like a man. His Voice blooms ... like a seed. Chosen for a moment to release ... and to blossom." Each image-packed page was full of turmoil for the characters and for my own feelings of uncertainty and questioning in life. I was challenged, encouraged, and hope-filled by the end.

~Gene Kent, COO, Speak Up Ministries, Co author of *Staying Power: Building a Stronger Marriage When Life Sends Its Worst.*

David Marsh brings the story of Noah alive. A masterful writer, David captures each person's likely emotions and experiences, drawing you into a deeper understanding of this important biblical event. I highly recommend it.

~Mark Savage, pastor, speaker, and author of *No More Perfect Marriages*

A Christian author crafts his message from the vision God stirs within his heart. His hope is to expand on the vision, capturing the reader through words and images that inspire a journey filled with experiencing God's presence-- and hope. Waterborne sparks one of these exceptional adventures and leaves the reader wanting more. Now I can imagine the story from a perspective I had never considered. Step into this fresh re-telling with David Marsh and enjoy the possibilities as they unfold.

~Scott Schuler, author, *Why Can't I Get This Jesus Thing Right* and disciple guide, *Getting It Right With Jesus*

Also by David J. Marsh

FICTION

The Confessions of Adam

NONFICTION

*A Conversation on Genesis 2-4:
Study Guide*

AUTHOR OF "THE CONFESSIONS OF ADAM"
DAVID J. MARSH

WATERBORNE
CHRONICLE OF THE CLAN OF NOAH

WATERBORNE

Chronicle of the Clan of Noah

A Novel

David J. Marsh

Bold Vision Books
PO Box 2011
Friendswood, TX 77549

Copyright ©David J. Marsh 2023

ISBN 978-1-946708-97-7
Library of Congress Control Number 2023946450

All rights reserved.
Published by Bold Vision Books, PO Box 2011, Friendswood, Texas 77549
www.boldvisionbooks.com

Published in cooperation with Joelle Delbourgo Associates Literary Agency
Edited by Cynthia Ruchti
Cover Art by Emily Quick
Cover Design by Amber Weigand-Buckley, Barefaced Media
Interior design by kae Creative Solutions
Author photo credit: Julia Peterson

Published in the United States of America.

This book is a work of fiction. Names, characters, places, and incidents are either products of the author's imagination or are used fictitiously and any resemblance to actual persons, living or dead, business establishments, events or locales is purely coincidental.

All rights reserved. No part of this publication may be reproduced, stored in a retrieval system, or transmitted in any form or by any means—electronic, mechanical, photocopy, recording, or any other—except for brief quotations in printed reviews, without the prior permission of the publisher.

For

Julia, Lydia, and Tate

&

For

CKM

All of Life. Together.

Author's Note

Noah's ark is familiar to us. We've heard the story. We've seen it portrayed in art and film. Some of us had toys based on the story. Parents have used it as a theme to decorate nurseries. A replica stands in northern Kentucky. This fact of uber-familiarity is what drew me to the narrative.

Like many of you, the story was for me commonplace, like Adam and Eve or David and Goliath; it was a story I'd seemingly always known. At the same time, I'd always been on the outside of the story, hearing and seeing it through a parent, Sunday school teacher, or filmmaker. There had always been a narrator between me and the rising waters.

On 10 March 2018 I wrote the first lines that would become Waterborne. While working through a writing exercise I first stepped inside this narrative and channeled the voice of Shem. *This is my father's story. He is dead. He'll not be telling it. I'll begin by saying, at the start, none of us knew what a cubit was.*

Though they wouldn't survive future edits, with these first few lines this story that was so familiar as to be lifeless, lifted its head, unfolded itself, and stood up off the page.

We have no biblical record of what Noah, his wife, or his family thought, said, or felt. Half of them aren't offered names. The events are laid out more as reportage than narrative. The inquisitive reader must take the initiative to imagine.

Most helpful to such imagining is the fact that humans have remained the same throughout the ages. Our span of needs, emotions, concerns, and joys--though triggered by a different set of circumstances--remain the same.

So, let us lift the report from the pages of the sacred text, join it with our shared knowledge of the human heart, and step together inside the clan of Noah.

dm
Avon, IN
May 2023

The Clan of Noah
at the time of these events

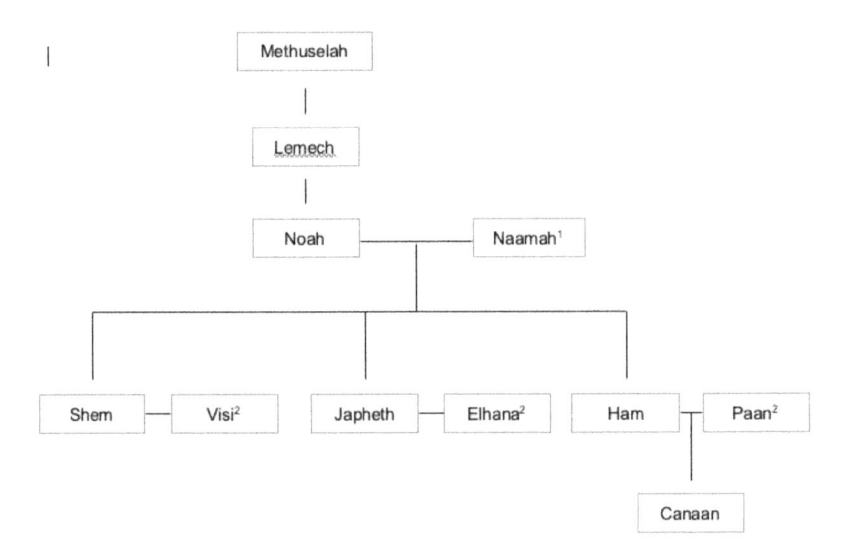

```
                    Methuselah
                        |
                     Lemech
                        |
              Noah ─────────── Naamah[1]
                        |
     ┌──────────────────┼──────────────────┐
  Shem ─ Visi[2]    Japheth ─ Elhana[2]   Ham ─ Paan[2]
                                            |
                                         Canaan
```

[1] Name not certain from the biblical text.

[2] Name not given in biblical text.

We carried Noah's lifeless, withered body in a sling of linen. We stretched the cloth between two of the shepherd's staffs he'd used—one before the waters came and the other after. We left at dawn, the first morning of the new moon. We walked from Babel to the mountains of Ararat.

We climbed and stood in a huddle at the base of the moored and weather-beaten ark. In the shadow of the great hull, we coated his body in a mud of spices, rolled him in the linen, and layered him in pitch. Splitting and removing the rock, we formed a cave under the craft. There we laid his body behind the stone.

But before.
Before this we each spent time with him.

Some of us spent the dawn and first light of day. Some entered his tent at dusk carrying a lamp of oil and passed the night hours. Some sat as the heat of the afternoon built—and with it the odor of the dying. Some took but a few moments to stand just inside his tent, unable to do more. One of us could only lift the flap of goat hide and look inside, unnoticed.

Each of us did with these last hours as we would. As we could.

Some listened. Some spoke. Some sat in silence. Some held tumblers of wine to his lips to ease his pain. All of us looked and saw his body, wrung of labor, void of strength. The prophet, patriarch, and shipbuilder. He who had once seen the vision and heard the words of The Maker, now half blind and deaf.

What follows is our story. Each of us has borne the story—of these last days, indeed, but more so. The story

Shem/Visi | Japheth/Elhana | Ham/Paan

of all that brought us here. The story that yields such an ending.

Together we pause, turn, and look over our shoulders.

Here is what we see.

W

Shem/Visi | Japheth/Elhana | Ham/Paan

Noah walked with God

G.6.9

BEFORE: **A Great Storehouse of Wood**

Shem, Son of Noah

I am Shem. Noah was my father. The man who rescued humanity now lay shriveled and dying. I sat on a stool at the edge of his bed. I'd served him in so many ways. How could I serve him now? Perhaps I could humor the old prophet, push some energy into his ribs. Perhaps I could revive his limbs with that skill for which I am known–retelling shared pasts. I knew he relished one memory more than any other.

Do you remember, Father?

He did not stir.

They couldn't silence you.

I watched his chest fall. Then rise.

The bloodpriest clutched a fistful of Father's beard and held a wrist blade to his gut. A crowd had formed to hear the prophecy but now remained to watch. The bloodpriest screamed he'd lay Father open if he didn't stop.

Father paused.

Then uttered another sentence.

And with his belly pressed against the blade, one more.

Spitting curses, calling down dark winds, the bloodpriest pulled Father to the ground while the marketlord held the tip of a spear at the base of his spine. Father's chin in the dirt, he ceased his speech. He laid still. The crowd's murmurs quieted. At last they allowed him to stand. They believed they had silenced him.

Shem/Visi | Japheth/Elhana | Ham/Paan

W

Golden sculptures of Cain stood along the river's edge. It was believed he had made a new way for all mankind. The Creator of Independence. Cain's act of will, his silencing of Abel, was hailed as the greatest act. The elevation of man toward becoming a god. From this came all else. From this came the drive to satisfy every appetite, to obey every desire. Lusts were fed while weaklings starved. Firstborn sons were given his name—wailing infants, raised to master sorcery and scandal. The old, disfigured by violence and vice, died alone in their beds, collapsed in the streets, slumped to tavern floors. Their funeral pyres gave light to festivals where the mark of Cain was tattooed on the most devout.

You spoke loud and often against the Faith of Cain. Do you remember, Father? You spoke of The Maker, of how The Maker had seen Cain's act of evil, yet in mercy spared him.

He stirred only to lift a trembling hand from under the quilted wool and stroke his beard.

I did not tell Father that we, being of Noah's clan, of his loins, had received our portion of the hatred he earned. The Effort was all we had—all any of us had—and his bold speech made certain of it.

Shem/Visi | Japheth/Elhana | Ham/Paan

Father said it came to him long before he spoke of it. Perhaps he'd first read of it in the dusk sky as the last light drained from the clouds. Perhaps it came to him in the still of an afternoon's heat, a stir of air circling his elbow. Perhaps upon the pasture after a dark night's keep it overflowed the edge of the horizon, rode the blush of dawn.

For me, for us, it started at the end of a workday, now long past.

Japheth and I had spent the day moving herds, finding pasture, ensuring water. We had gathered at the well to drink and to wash. Our wives and mother had been at work, too. We breathed deep the aroma of the stew pot over the fire and the brown loaves warming on the oven stones. Visi, her hair cut shorter than mine, her damp cloak tied up to reveal her muscular arms and legs, had just returned from the riverbank, from bathing the donkeys. Of all she did to help, was this not surely the least?

We spoke as family does, of the day just ending, of the day ahead—we spoke with no idea our days were about to be altered forever. It was Paan who first spotted him. All conversation stopped as we turned to follow her gaze.

Father came toward us from across the distant pasture. From over the farthest knoll—his shoulders, knees, then all of him came into view. Walking, looking at the ground, each step taken as if treading the edge of a cliff. He didn't look up as he neared or when he stopped in front of us and spoke.

Be still. The Maker gives numbers. Not words. Numbers. The lines are drawn, the plumb is set. 300. 50. 30. Bring me slate and flint.

I ran and found two slates and a flint outside the shepherds' quarters and held them out to him.

Shem/Visi | Japheth/Elhana | Ham/Paan

These will not hold but the start of it. To the quarry. Go.

The start of what? This question we muttered—Ham, Japheth, and I as we walked in pools of torchlight, our supper awaiting us. In the quarry we collected and strapped stacks of slate to the backs of the donkeys. We did not know that this labor was but part of the start of which he spoke. A beginning.

The beginning.

Father was prone to turns of fancy, spirts of will. His commands often came with only a shift of his eyes, a sudden pull and weave of his hand into his beard. But this, *The Maker gives*, had the tone of more than opening a new pasture or extending last year's stone wall another thousand paces. Indeed, for three days Father took no sleep or food but remained hunched, bent to the ground. At night we took turns holding a lamp at his elbow. He left knee-prints of blood as he scratched on the slates the plans that would guide our work.

And change us all.

Shem/Visi l Japheth/Elhana l Ham/Paan

Three mornings later the rising sun cast our shadows as we stared at what he had done. He'd used all the slates we'd gathered from the quarry. He'd asked for not one more.

Is that a floor or a ceiling?
Rooms stacked three high?
Where will we uncover a stone for such a hoist?

We had built structures before but what these slates held made us wonder if he'd made an error. Or errors. As we looked at the slates and our understanding of the envisioned mass grew, so did our panic.

We passed the slates between us.

A door that hinges at the bottom and becomes a ramp?
Are we to harvest trees as we do wheat?

Father stood among us, the flint locked between his forefinger and thumb. *Ask your many questions. And when you have exhausted yourselves, know it is The Maker who speaks. He is in heaven, you are on earth. Let your words be few. For The Maker sees both the design of a boat and the unbowed soul of a man.*

Our questions slowed.

With these instructions came the cubit, a measure set at the length of Father's elbow to his longest fingertip. We made dozens of willow rods of this length. For nothing so large had ever been conceived, let alone built by the hands of men. Within days we'd felled the first few gopher trees.

For many evening meals thereafter we sat in a circle, the moon high overhead, and pulled splinters from our palms and forearms, flicking them into the fire. Bits of our labor caught spark and turned to cinder.

Shem/Visi | Japheth/Elhana | Ham/Paan

W

Only he had ever seen a structure built to travel atop water. He had once seen the ocean. None of us had seen such wonders. And none of us, him included, had ever seen a great rain. We knew only the fog and soaking mists that came with the planting season, or the heavy dews that coated and fell from the trees in late summer. When Father said the first words about the Effort, there was no experience from which to make a start. Nothing in our shared pasts to which we might lash the idea.

At first Visi and I hovered over him—oversight to keep his passion for the Effort from leaching all remaining strength from his bones. The day Father tore down the winepress to make room for the raising I realized there would be no talking him out of it. And after seeing the swollen results of Ham's attempt, I thought better of it altogether.

I'm sorry I have made them, I heard Father say as he split apart the last wooden vat.

He paused and looked out across the pasture, the villages and the rise of the city beyond. The tone of his words, the way they fell, caused me to pause. Such regret. Were these Father's words or words of The Maker? Surely such words were not aimed at simple vats for holding wine.

Do you remember, Father? Do you remember saying "I'm sorry I have made them" as you took down the winepress?

He laid still and opened his eyes. I waited a moment, and a few more.

Yes.

Where did you get such words?

His eyes had closed. I thought him asleep and was startled when he spoke. *The Maker told me of His regret over mankind. I was His echo.*

Shem/Visi | Japheth/Elhana | Ham/Paan

Father stood out among all other men. He laid a path of hope where there was none. Father's vision for the invisible, his grasp of the mystery—had it come of Lemech's blessing uttered over him at his birth?

This one will console us for the pain of our hands' work from the soil which the Lord cursed.

Perhaps these words were kept fresh by the years that followed under Methuselah's watchful eye.

Whether we had been of his loins or not, Father was one to be followed; so bright was his prophecy in the midst of the darkness that surrounded us.

Consolation comes in unimagined ways.

When The Maker speaks it is not in a voice like a man's. It is not a voice as you think of it, language spoken aloud, one you take in, one to which you listen. No, this voice blooms. It is as if the seed of it was long ago dropped into my ear and at the chosen moment released, clear and quiet. But why for me? And why for me alone?

He and I sat alone, first up for the day's work, the blush of dawn over the pasture and the pain of the previous day's labor rippling across his face. I had said nothing, made no comment, asked no questions. Father told me this, simply offered it up.

And again, as was so often, my father's words left me with none.

Shem/Visi I Japheth/Elhana I Ham/Paan

As the beams ascended, we discovered the bowl of the structure acted as a kind of horn for our words. Under the midday sun Ham asked Japheth and me, just above a whisper, the question we were all thinking.

When the waters come, if they come, who do you think will be taken inside?

The sound of work ceased and silence fell. Father looked down at us from atop the first floor, his three sons standing in our man-made shade.

Ham had not intended him to hear. At first Father appeared to be listening to us for the answer, but then he started to speak, halting—once, twice—as if whittling his message down to its finest point.

Me, your mother, and the six of you.

We waited for more, for the remainder of the list. Japheth lifted his hands, looked at us and back up at Father. The question needed to be asked, yes? Our grandparents? His and Mother's brothers and sisters perhaps?

Father waited with us, silent, his eyes looking to us as well. A moment came and went.

Nodding as if certain the question had been settled, he turned and lifted his blade to form another shim.

W

Within a dozen years we saw rising before us what deepest sleep could not conjure. We could not have built such a structure alone. Building the Effort became running a brisk trade. We dealt with all who would deal with us, often several at once.

One wealthy tradesman, imagining his opportunity to strike a bargain, began to take Elhana as payment for supplies. His eyes wide, he ordered his servant to loop a rope around her wrists and put a ring in her nose. The greedy fool couldn't have known Father viewed our wives as his own daughters.

We heard her cry out and came running with Japheth from around the Effort. Before the servant could follow the command, Father had seen what was happening. Without a word he pulled the tradesman from his wagon and beat him until he could barely stand. He then threw the man back atop the still-loaded wagon on which he'd come, handed the trembling servant the reins, and pointed the startled oxen back toward the valley.

As the oxen hied back down the path they had come, Father turned to us with a stony calm. *Let light shine in the darkness.*

Back at my chore, chisel in hand, I was grateful I had put Visi on the task of mixing pitch, that I'd hidden her allure under layers of soot. At night when we'd lie together, she had none of the scent or sensitivity of a woman. Her calloused hands and sap-stained arms, the hard muscle of her neck and shoulders, as well as her stench of smoke and sweat—these would have attracted no man, no matter his intent.

Shem/Visi | Japheth/Elhana | Ham/Paan

We had ceased to travel alone when going into the villages. We went in pairs, and more if possible. We ceased taking the women at all. We were harassed, threatened, cursed, heckled, and spat upon--often in combination. To go alone would be a fool's risk. To take our wives would be folly.

But the last time we went into the village--my brothers and I with Father--we experienced a turn. Our craft on the pasture had incited a change. We were moved from harassed to holy. A new darkness.

I will tell it as it happened.

We walk through the narrow streets under the hot sun. A few men begin to gather, keeping pace with us. This is not new. Once they amass, we will stop. Father will speak with them, try once more to warn them of the coming waters. Long ago we memorized the insults they will return. But today we walk and there are more than usual. A mass of men is forming, women and children too--a crowd larger than ever before is closing in behind us.

We grow unsure which way to go. Each corner we turn there are more. The entire village is turning out as if they were expecting us. They stream in from the sides, pushing in upon us. Shops go silent and empty. Craftsmen cease their work. As they come, they call yet more to gather. Have we made a grave error, the four of us coming into the village together?

At that moment, in the street ahead, the bloodpreist appears. He walks toward us. Our path forward is ending. We are encircled by the bulging crowd. We slow to a stop.

A chant we've never heard rises and sounds, echos all around us. I feel the voice of the crowd, the rumble in my chest. We are trapped. The bloodpriest steps forward. He

Shem/Visi | Japheth/Elhana | Ham/Paan

lifts his sharpened scepter. The crowd goes silent. A pure silence, the sort found in the desert at dawn.

The absence of the chant is a fleeting relief. The silence offers little comfort. We wait as the bloodpriest approaches us, his scepter still high in command of the crowd. He stands behind Father and begins to lower his scepter. We watch in disbelief as the bloodpriest lowers his scepter and taps Father on the back of the neck, drawing a sliver of blood at the base of his skull. The oppressive silence continues as the bloodpriest moves between us and taps each of us, in succession, on the neck. We know the meaning. No words are uttered. For any living creature tapped in this way by the bloodpriest's scepter is made holy. In this way, gods are made by men.

At the last tap, upon my neck, a horn sounds. A solitary blast from somewhere above us. The crowd pulls back and separates. A clearing forms, and as far as we can see a path opens up before us. All–men, women, children–fall to their knees in worship of us. Still silent. Faces and palms in the dirt. It is when the crowd separates and kneels we see what we'd missed. Stones have been stacked to form an altar in the shape of the Effort. A pair of children, male and female, have been strapped to it.

We are standing in our own shrine.

My brothers and I look at each other, unsure what to do next.

Father is not.

He turns.

And runs.

Cutting this corner then that, we follow him though the village, past the bowed worshippers lining the streets, their palms and chins to the earth.

We run out of the village and across the valley.

We leap into and swim the river.

Shem/Visi | Japheth/Elhana | Ham/Paan

We sprint onto the high pastures.

We keep pace as if a cold wind blows at our backs, hurtling us home. We run until at last we reach the perch of the Effort and collapse at the base of its rising walls.

From that day, the Effort became a public wonder.

The craft of the gods.

People came from afar to see it. Hillsides of encamped spectators watch us coat in pitch the form we'd raised, its mass spread over the crest of our highest pasture. They raise their voices to accompany our work.

Father's name in children's chants.

Profane praise in poet's songs.

I carved my name into one of the beams. Chips of gopher wood bounced off my shoulders and chest.

SHEM

    Why did I do this?
    Was I claiming the Effort? Permanently attaching myself to this work? Was I putting my name on the craft, a sort of builder's mark?
    I didn't have these thoughts until after I'd finished. Had I considered before doing it, I may not have done so.
    I would not have done so.
    I'm certain.

Shem/Visi l Japheth/Elhana l Ham/Paan

How will we gather the animals from the land?
Across the evening's fire I posed the question we all had but none spoke. As I had not told anyone I was going to ask, their eyes met mine with equal parts curiosity and concern before shifting to Father and awaiting his answer.

Father looked up at me. He stood and looked into the fire.

I've been told an answer to your question. They will come to us. Just as they came to Adam for their names, they will come to me for their rescue.

We stared at each other, our lips parted, no words. Had Father just answered my question by comparing himself to Adam of Eden?

He had. Was this hubris or affiliation?

Late that night Visi and I talked.

He's joining himself to Adam, she said. *He was telling you how the animals will come. He's also suggesting he and Adam will one day stand together, fall as a pair from the lips of oracles and from the nibs of scribe's pens.*

I look back now and she was right. A mass of creatures did gather, just as he said they would.

And I hear Adam of Eden and my father mentioned together more often now than ever.

Shem/Visi | Japheth/Elhana | Ham/Paan

In the bright morning sun, under a clear blue sky, Father dropped open the ramp that led up into the Effort. The underside of it fully coated in pitch, the sound of it hitting the dry earth cracked across the valley like the felling of a great oak. Every creature went silent, lifted its head, and turned to look. Then, like a great pool breached, the mass of creatures cleaved the encampment on the hillside and began to funnel toward Father who stood with his staff raised high atop the only remaining lattice.

W

We did nothing to wrangle or coax the beasts. Nothing. Each pair of creatures moved through the inside of the craft and found the space best fashioned to suit its needs. The design upon the slates had been so thorough, we had built each a place. We did nothing more than open it up to them and step out of their path toward it.

At the edge of the parade, under the plume of dust they were raising into the midday sky, I looked down at a discarded slate at my feet. My father's scratches and scribbles—numbers and measures from the mind of The Maker. Through us The Maker had fashioned the materials of His making into the greatest grange ever built.

There was no other explanation.

The next morning, we too were shut inside. The ramp we'd used was sealed behind us. Japheth, Ham, and I walked every aisle, pinned every cage, latched every crate. So was our introduction to tending and keeping this huffing, snarling, bellowing remnant of life.

Shem/Visi l Japheth/Elhana l Ham/Paan

Visi, Wife of Shem

I stepped into the tent and stood in the pale midday light. I said nothing. My husband's father opened his eyes and let them fall shut before speaking.

I do not like this parade of visitors. But what choice am I given? Part of the life of the living is the observation of the dying. But you, you're the reporter of what happened, the collector of keeps, skilled in raising and turning flesh into meat. And your beauty is like sunlight in this cave.

I'd been summed up in three easy phrases, and a fourth. I could argue with none of it. And even if I could, a man should be forgiven much when speaking from the bed on which he'll die.

I was a lover of animals when I met Shem. As a little girl, I began an unknowing apprenticeship. Escaping my father's fists and heavy breath in the moonlight as well as the pit left by my mother's absence, I roamed among the creatures of pastures and pens. I sought out the beasts of fields and forests. I slept among them. They became at ease in my presence. I was somehow qualifying myself. But here I was turned from a lover and observer into a keeper of creatures. I learned husbandry by marriage into this clan.

Did Shem mention the donkeys? How we put them in service of the slates? How we led them from spot to spot? How they slept in the sun when free of the slates? How we, in our constant fatigue of labor, were jealous of them, this trio in slumber?

The slates that held the lines, angles, and joints, these were their unique burden. Lesser donkeys carried bundles of wheat, rolls of wool, heaps of sticks. The slate donkeys grew stout, their legs and loins bulging with muscle.

The Slate Donkeys.

This is what we came to call them. I spent an afternoon now and again washing the donkeys—a fistful of cattails, pails of river water. Shem called me silly and asked why I bothered. I didn't know then why I did it either, why I bathed them. But now that I've written it, I know. Yes. Every creature called into labor needs care.

We watched Noah create towering forms that stood at the sides of the Effort, tree limbs stripped bare, squared, balanced, and lashed together. High above our heads he walked on this lattice as if he were walking on the threshing floor. We wondered--speaking with our hands over our mouths--where a keeper of herds and vineyards, a grower of wheat, barley, and rye, obtains such craft?

Noah owned a dozen herdsman's staffs, each with a hook, knob, or prod; some shaped for driving, others for lifting to safety, yet others for beating back wild creatures with a taste for raw lamb or goat. These, the tools of a lifetime, he tossed aside in favor of adzes and hammers with granite heads, some the size of a child's fist, others as large as bread loaves.

With the scratches upon the slates came a knowledge. Surely a man is not given a vision from The Maker without instruction on making it so? What we saw on the slates were notes on what was to be. How it was to be--this was grafted into Noah's bones, instilled in his frame as he knelt under The Maker's revelation.

No one told me this was how such a mystery happened. This came to be my belief.

Shem/**Visi** | Japheth/Elhana | Ham/Paan

As work on the craft increased, the work of building onto Noah and Naamah's house was soon abandoned altogether. Their home was a cluster of buildings between which stood porticos. This was where our clan lived among their fields, vineyards, and pastures. The door in the gate to the main house was said to be made of wood from the edge of Eden.

The added rooms were to have been for Shem and me, as we were the most recent to be joined together. To *become one flesh*, as Lemech said. A home of our own, a place we would bring our own children into—the clan of Noah and all its prosperity was to be ours, mine.

A home at last.

A life both set and safe.

A life only started, interrupted by a great starting over.

Shem/**Visi** | Japheth/Elhana | Ham/Paan

Every timber used to build the Effort was coated in pitch. When hot, pitch gives off a dark and pungent smoke that smells of the heated sap of cedar and burning citrus. When it cools it forms a thick scab. All around the Effort it dripped and cooled, covering the grass. It made for a slippery walk when the morning dews came. In the midday heat we lifted our smocks to our knees to keep cool while the bottoms of our feet turned black.

Ours was not the first and only use of pitch. Shem told me flaming balls of pitch had been used in battle. When slung, their trails of black smoke gave the illusion of fiery rocks in mid-air. Upon impact, flaming bits splattered every surface, setting entire villages ablaze. This caused me to wonder ... did those who watched us work, and saw our great pots of boiling pitch, wonder if we were preparing for war?

Twice we tried to count the number of people among the tents on the hillside--those who had come to *watch the gods build their chest.* The first time the number we settled on was 10,000. A handful of moons later we couldn't agree on a number. I'll write 40,000, but I've no confidence.

A fire starter was hired to ensure nightly fires were lit and torches placed on every third beam or joist. In construction by night, the craft took on the appearance of a great cavern under exploration.

Later, when we were afloat, I saw soot stains in the high reaches of the hull from those night lights.

w

Spiders the size of a man's hand and covered in fur. Snakes the girth of a cedar trunk. Insects whose wings hummed at the pitch of a woman's scream. These were a few of the creatures that caused mothers to pull their children close.

The animals came to us. All came in pairs as they filed toward the craft. Many were caked with dirt--their legs and underbodies. From what distances had they come? From the young of those with tails like a stone ridge, to the tiger whose teeth hang outside her jaw, to the sharp-beaked hummingbird who snatches insects in mid-flight; their sounds were the brush of claws or paws against the dry earth, the stir and lift of wings, and the whisk of a tail in the still, hot air.

Each made a single call, according to its kind as it stepped onto the ramp. Noah studied their form and in return called each pair by name, spelling it aloud as they descended into the cool shadows of the hold. Most we had never seen before. More knowledge given to Noah in the mysterious exchange.

Pairs of waterfowl and river birds descended upon the top of the craft--webbed feet and hooked beaks, wings spread wide waiting for the waters. By the end of the second day the craft was speckled with their thick, white paste, down, and feathers. Noah coated the bottoms of his sandals in pitch and embedded slivers of slate so he could walk across the upper-most deck.

Two of the three Slate Donkeys were the last to walk up the ramp. No burden rested on their bare backs save that of the afternoon shadows. The third donkey had dropped dead--under the last season's new moon, his eyes wide, sniffing the evening breeze out of the east.

As this last pair descended, a cloud slipped between us and the setting sun.

The breeze fell still.

> We looked up at the only cloud in the sky—formed of white scalloped edges, ascending in a gray column, its top flattening against the heavens.

W

Shem/**Visi** I Japheth/Elhana I Ham/Paan

None of us slept that final night, the craft full of noise and motion. The fire starter came, climbed the ramp tracked with dirt, grass, and ordure, and placed lit lamps on each floor.

His eyes wide at the collection we had amassed, he said he'd be back in the morning to collect the lamps as well as his pay. Noah told him to take the remaining sheep in the fold. We never saw him again.

We gathered in the weak morning light. We stood just inside the craft, at the mouth of the ramp. Gusts of wind spun around and into the Effort. Leaves took to the air like flocks of birds. The first drops of rain passed over us and hit the pasture, then a few more, and yet more--the rhythm of the water building--as if the sky was pelting the earth in a rising anger.

Beyond the ramp and the pasture I saw a throng, a multitude of villagers with their flocks and wagons, caught in what they couldn't conceive--the start of a mid-morning deluge. More streamed from the city beyond--night watchmen dressed for war, nursemaids with children hanging from their hips, merchants with bags of wool slung over their backs, mongers pushing carts following mongers who had abandoned theirs--a bulging horde united in a panic that propelled them toward us.

As we watched and pointed, the ramp lifted from the earth and hovered. We stumbled back, further into the lower hold as a plume of grass and cinder swirled up and around it. The ramp fell back to earth and we were given a final look at the pasture which was about to be breached by the now rioting mass. The ramp lifted again, hovering as before, then, in one great gust, it slammed shut. The entire craft shuddered as we were showered with wet grit. We cowered behind the ramp, now a wall which separated us from the throng, the multitude trampling the pasture and the life we'd come to call the Once Past.

Shem/**Visi** | Japheth/Elhana | Ham/Paan

Japheth, Son of Noah

I knelt at Ab Noah's bed and looked at him, unsure what to say. As I stared and stalled, the silence widened and morphed from a void I needed to fill into a gem that needed protection and care.

Neither he nor I said anything, yet we found ourselves working side-by-side, as we had so many times before, this time working together to preserve this supple silence that had risen between us. An eddy of peace. A bend of quiet. Both had been rare in the old man's life.

But alas.

I felt myself pull a breath. I heard myself start to speak. I heard myself say, simply, ignoring the care we'd put into the moment...

You have done well.

He looked at me.

My words were not worthy of the silence they had broken. I'd said this phrase as if I could offer such a judgment, bestow such a commendation. As if such a statement was needed and would be more of a salve than the quiet we had procured.

At once I wished to eviscerate my vowels, castrate my consonants. To build back all that had been knocked down with my puny utterance. But the words had come, in all their frailty and wooliness. The best I could now do was to say nothing. To say nothing more. To set myself to the task of restoring a new silence.

A right and fine response to all he had done.

Of the tens of thousands in the valley and the countless thousands living in the hill lands, many came to look at the first wooden beams hewn and laid among the flocks in our eastern pasture. The first beams of what would be the form, the cradle in which the Effort would be built.

When they asked, Ab told them. He answered with the prophecy he would repeat until the first pillared cloud crested the horizon.

The Maker has limited His patience. He will tarry with men only a little longer before He rends the heavens and splits open the earth. There will be an overflow covering all that breathes. All that wears flesh and all that is green will be washed away.

I am building a water chest.

When Ab spoke of the future some listened. They listened to his words, the tone and shape of them. His was rare speech, forms of phrase heard nowhere else. Some came and listened over and over, as if they might become one of us. But in the end, the revelation of what was to come, the vision and voice, became for them only a new amusement.

Come! Hear the prophet Noah, the seer-shepherd who trades not only in wool and wood, but words!

He speaks for a new god!

Ab knelt under the hot sun composing a crude chant--mumbles and grunts accompanied by the scratch of his flint against the slates. Each drawing revealed a section, an angle, a view. He numbered and lettered each slate. The slates, when stacked, were as tall as two men.

Ab sorted them, tied them in bundles with hemp, and loaded them onto the backs of the donkeys. We led the beasts about and he laid out the slates for our reference wherever needed.

Each day Ab's father's father sat on a stump and watched. His age hung upon him like a stained and wrinkled cloak. Its long stem tucked under his belt, a palm leaf arched up and over him for shade. His face framed in dozens of braids of long white hair, the glare of his one remaining eye lay fixed, watery, unblinking on our labor.

Methuselah.

"When he is gone it shall be sent."

This, the meaning of his name, pulled our saws through the timber and quickened the strokes of our hammers.

Ab directed our cutting and stacking of timbers. We made lifts of hemp and stone weight. He oversaw our trimming and joining of each rafter and joist. He could fashion a joining peg with four strokes of a blade and drive it in three blows. And by the end so could we. He made craftsmen of us all, passing on to us skills we didn't know he had.

Learning new skills isn't without pain. Stripping bark, I slid my hatchet down a log. The blade bounced off a knot and found my thumb, clipping it off at the first knuckle. These years later, the numb scar that forms the stub looks like the surface of an angry sea.

Inside we worked shoulder-to-shoulder on our hands and knees, according to the slates, dividing and dividing

Shem/Visi I **Japheth**/Elhana I Ham/Paan

again each floor into stalls, coops, dens, and warrens. We unearthed the root ball of a tree, hoisted it whole, and lowered it into a barrel in the bottom hold.

A place for nests and hives, said Ab.

We cut kerfs in green planks. With hammers and chisels we joined beams fitting square pegs of seasoned oak into round holes of gopher wood. The gopher tightened around the peg as it dried. A bond like no other.

Nay. A bond like ours.

Ab was not always present. Building the Effort was only part of his work. He had another craft. The craft of forming speech to gain the attention of heathens and fiends—to distract them from their wiles, excesses, and abuses long enough to wedge among them a warning, reinsert the long-forgotten Maker.

Ab told us what he saw on his prophet's travels, in the midst of their revel and his rant. And even as he did so, his countenance was that of a man hearing a report spoken aloud for the first time.

I have seen a mid-winter festival where girls are taken from their milk-mothers' knees and divided into harems.

Girls, gathered together, their ankles and wrists lashed with rope, are given strong drink and forced to lie down. I've heard their screams as they were branded with the mark of their harem, and I've seen their tear-stained faces as they were led away to replace women found dead in birthing shacks or given in sacrifice the year before.

Yes, Ab spoke of what he saw on his travels. He paused and hovered over the images as he put them in words for the first time.

I witnessed sport. Sport where orphaned boys are made to fight blinded bears. Even so, I stood among them. I stood among the men who invented such games and those who wager upon them. I told them. Man destroys mankind. Man destroys the beasts that roam the earth. The waters will come, I said. An end to destruction. A remnant of creation will be lifted out.

One of the orphans took my hand and listened until it was his turn with the bear.

Elhana stood to leave when Ab was finished, a look on her face as if she was carrying the full weight of such dreads.

She turned to us. *Under every setting sun, under every rising moon, a thousand abuses, ten-thousand evils. What is worse than mankind's treatment of its own? The question knows its answer.*

Late that night, thinking upon what we'd heard from Ab, I had a realization, a coming to.

The Maker was not destroying mankind; mankind was destroying itself. The waters were being brought to save a remnant, to save a few of us before we were all, each one of us, swallowed up by our invented horrors. And there was the shock of it—the waters were not a pending judgment but a looming mercy.

Ensuring we were alone, I voiced my conclusion to Shem.

You are slow to see, Japheth. Yes, of course, this is the fact of it.

I assumed, from then after, we all saw the Effort this way. And perhaps we will, one day find our way to such a coda. But we are still doing so.

Ab told me as a child he once tried to hold water in his hands. This was his earliest memory. Standing on fat, wobbly legs at the edge of the village pool, his mother and father close by, cooling themselves in the heat of the day. He told me his memory of growing frustrated and soon bursting into a tantrum, his mother unable to console him, as the water drained between his palms and interwoven fingers, dribbling onto the ground at his feet.

 He said this was a memory that often came to him in glimpses, in frets of anxiety.

 A boy seeking to master water, he said.

 The grass around the Effort long ago worn away, the slates lay scattered in dirt among wood shavings, scrap, and broken tools. It took nearly two thousand steps to walk around the base of the craft. I made this walk once, early one morning with one of my doves perched on my shoulder, not long before the waters came. Ab made the walk every morning. A survey of the previous day's work, studying, inspecting, one hand on the Effort, the other pulled in close, curled at his side. Seeking to master water.

I've mentioned one of my birds. As a boy, and later as a young man, I raised doves and pigeons. I taught them to fly and return to me. I had a pair of ravens as well. They ate from the palm of my hand as I brushed the dust from their ebony feathers.

I asked Ab if I could take them with me aboard the Effort. At first I wasn't sure he heard me. I repeated the question. After a long pause, during which he looked to the sky and appeared to be listening well beyond where my question ended, his eyes met mine.

Yes, he said.

When I returned home that evening, I told Elhana. *I asked him today and he said yes.*

Elhana looked at me. *Pigeons and ravens? We have room for pigeons and ravens but not—*

The halt of her words hung like the next anticipated blow of a mallet gone silent.

A few minutes passed. I told her my conclusion. *Mankind destroys itself, Elhana. We are being lifted out, saved—a remnant.*

She shook her head. *No—I know those words. That is Shem speaking. That is Shem's cold logic on your lips.*

I fell silent.

I am He who made Adam. I made you also, and your donkeys, and this place in which you've led your donkeys. And this is how I will show Myself. You will see all you have known washed away. You and those of your house will live on, a remnant borne upon the waters.

Ab repeated The Maker's words to us one last time before the rains came.

He said they tasted like honey as their sounds formed on his tongue.

He later said the weight of these words sat like slugs of lead in his cheeks.

He said when spoken they left a bitter smoke against the back of his throat.

He said he'd never had a vision of The Maker. And he'd long feared such a sight.

He said he'd once asked The Maker, in a trembling stutter, to leave him alone, to let him be. He said he knew The Maker had heard his petition but had kept pursuing him—sometimes as a raptor eyes its prey, but more often as a doe nudges her newborn fawn, still wet from birth, to stand.

At the edge of the pasture I spotted the stump where Methuselah had sat each day and watched us work. It was empty, on its side, the grass worn away where he'd rested his feet. Under my breath I uttered the meaning of his name.

I said it once more, aloud, my eyes turned from the stump toward the sky.

"When he is gone it shall be sent."

The next morning the rains came, first in drops, then in gushes, flattening the tall grasses of our pasture into hammered mats.

As the waters rose, so rose the sounds of battle for the few remaining pieces of dry ground.

Perhaps the chaos was no greater than it had ever been. Only wetter.

Elhana, Wife of Japheth

I went out of obligation, after dark, hoping he'd be asleep. I stood just inside the flap of his tent, pregnant. All day I'd felt the child churn inside me, now I felt nothing. I feared the death in the air might be riding my breath, each rise of my chest a brume to my unborn.

Noah did not open his eyes, he made no move but to untuck his arm and point a bony, gnarled finger toward me.

You and I are the only ones who conceive what happened. Don't tell the others I said this. You saw and you felt. You know the weight of water.

I didn't answer him.

I didn't answer because I hadn't come for an exchange of words with him. And I didn't answer because such truth doesn't need a response. I turned and left his tent, letting him speak for us both.

Shem/Visi | Japheth/**Elhana** | Ham/Paan

They could have made Noah their prophet-king. They could have crowned him and raised a new nation round about him. They could have cast golden statues in his likeness. They could have written what he said in ink, on hide, or chiseled it into stone.

Instead, he was their favorite madman.

They invited him to their orgies, to sit beside their pools of perry and mead, to gorge himself at their feasts. And he went. He stood awash in the sweat and steam of every dark invention of their desire and spoke words from The Maker. They pointed and laughed, clapped and asked for more. They asked him to repeat over and over the riddle about a change in the weather.

The prophecy, the vision, the voice. Among the givers and ghouls, the sorcerers and seers, he cut through the thick, unseen energies around us. No other voice told of water and wind. And images scratched into slate became a structure raised in wood.

As I watched what was happening around me, I began to believe the mocking crowds bore a seed of truth when they said, *he speaks for a new god.*

Shem/Visi I Japheth/**Elhana** I Ham/Paan

Strangers to each other, one-by-one Visi, Paan, and I had married into a family where The Maker spoke in woodcraft.

The three of us rose together. We worked together. Pressing clay to the inside of baskets and setting them to dry in the sun, we formed hundreds of basins to hold what Noah called "rain-water." We combed and rolled wool for our common need. We made plans for a life we couldn't imagine.

And we watched the mother of our husbands—both the work of her hands and the cast of her eyes—for a hint of what should come next. For when each task was done, when each sun was set, when our anxieties rose, we followed not Noah, but Naamah.

Shem/Visi I Japheth/**Elhana** I Ham/Paan

F or many days and nights after the tradesman's ropes were cut from my wrists, unease and fear rattled through me. The thought of nearly being given over—I knew what being sold could mean. Stories were told among women.

I also knew we were said to be building an escape from such evils.

And the thought came to me—had Noah saved me once only to save me yet again?

Shem/Visi | Japheth/**Elhana** | Ham/Paan

Three floors. These were reserved for those who would come to believe, along with their livestock and grain. This was the assumption I made. This was the assumption we all made. What else would we do with such space?

We would save animals while women and children drowned. This was the answer. This was the fact none of us spoke aloud.

There, I've written it. The old wound seeps again.

We wondered between us. Had we married into a salvation or a madness? Perhaps both?

Again, we worked toward a future we couldn't imagine. One we dared not try to. We rendered beeswax and poured candles. Thousands of candles. The three of us endured swarm and sting in exchange for the promise of future light.

Trust and love. In what order does this pair arrive? Is one the result of the other? These were my thoughts one evening as Japheth came to bed smelling of wood smoke and sweat, his youthful, hairless face streaked with dirt, gopher wood shavings littering his hair. I demanded he go bathe. He did, but not before pulling me close against him and putting a thumbprint of pitch on the back of my hand.

  I looked down at it after he'd left. This playful stamp. This symbol of the Effort's burden.

W

Shem/Visi I Japheth/**Elhana** I Ham/Paan

One of my tasks was to feed Methuselah. As the sun burned overhead, I approached the elder with a platter of raw spinach and two dried fishes. As I'd done a thousand times before, I laid the offering on his lap, across his thin legs and bony knees.

He didn't move, his concentration remained on the Effort. He only stroked the back of my hand with one pointed finger, his brittle and yellowed fingernail signaling unspoken gratitude.

One man pursues his vision of owning herds, of driving flocks, of building stalls that will cover the earth.

Another man is driven to craft a water chest, fitting it with stalls to fill with creatures, and traverse the earth.

One man chases a dream of wealth and the other a holy revelation. Can you or I divine the difference?

After thousands had been sold or traded for goods, the last few sheep from Noah's flock stood behind the slats of the fold, bleating in the dusk light. So possessed was Noah by his vision, I remember wondering...if we run out of goods to trade before the Effort is finished will Noah begin to broker in oaths for the servitude of his unborn grandchildren?

Ham, Son of Noah

As a child, my arms wrapped just above his knee, I looked up and watched the bounce of his chin. The deep rumble and roll of his voice excited me. A shiver just short of frightened.

When he sat, I watched his lips move. I stood behind him and wrapped my arms around his neck. I wove my fingers into his beard and felt the vibrations of his throat as he spoke—long before I knew the sounds washing over me were words. Long before there arose concern over the gritty power of the spoken.

In the bliss that is childhood, with false starts and missed vowels, I repeated the sounds he made, delighted to hear them, in a wispy tenor, come from my own lips.

breathes

split

green

cover

rend

I grew up with these words, and others like them, spoken, repeated, memorized, written with my fingertips in the dirt at his feet.

I would never have his depth of voice.

His was the mouth of The Maker.

It would have been easier to not return to this place, to have followed Paan's wishes. It would have been easier to not pick up this stylus and not write these words--to have let the old man die without my notice. But what these first sentences reveal is I made the harder choice.

He was the man from whose seed I had come, but he was a figure whom I most often saw at work or among a crowd--a keeper of herds turned builder of a structure of divine imagination. His sheepman's staff tossed into the grass, a finger pointed toward the sky, his knuckles white around a hammer's helve while in the throes of a prophet's rant, he proclaimed deserts turned oceans and a floating box, *a remnant of flesh and breath*.

I spoke to him one evening as we stacked firewood in the dying light of a red sky. As none of the others were willing, I felt compelled to ask him if he was sure, if he held even a small reserve of doubt about what he was asking of himself. What he was asking of us.

With a speed I'd never seen from him, he grasped a stave and struck me across the jaw. Pain shot up and coiled in my skull emitting a burst of light behind my watering eyes. Blood arched from my opened lip. My tongue probed my teeth, searching for any knocked loose. He looked at me as if I had cursed.

Shem/Visi | Japheth/Elhana | **Ham**/Paan

We paid in gold, and later livestock, and still later sacks of grain. In the end, when the sacks were gone, we paid with grain in bulk. We paid for single trees and entire stands of gopher wood, for the saws to cut them down, for the long-wagons, and for the hemp to weave into rope to attach the wagons to haul the timber.

Only the men with whom we traded dealt us no scorn. They were the strangers to get closest to the Effort. They would stare at it, wonder spanning their unblinking eyes, even the third or fourth time they'd seen it. Yet, not once, by either seller or supplier, were we asked for payment in the form of passage aboard our craft.

But for Methuselah, no one from the family ever came to see the Effort. Or to see us. The wider clan spoke with their absence. What was happening was too strange, even for the ties of blood—perhaps especially for the ties of blood.

A messenger did however come from my mother's parents. They offered Mother a place of respite. *A place away from the oppression and waste that has overtaken you.* Reports had traveled to their village of a herdsman called Noah who was trading sheep for trees, who was raising a boat amid the promise of rising waters.

Some moons later came another messenger, even as we were still entertaining the first. Again they offered, *our daughter and our sweet grandsons and their wives, a place to go if you wish to escape.*

We listened to each messenger. We asked them to repeat their missives—these offers of escape now from some imagined future escape.

Neither Mother, nor we, quickly dismissed the messengers.

Shem/Visi | Japheth/Elhana | **Ham**/Paan

We became craftsmen of every kind, workers in stone, wood, and hemp.

At midday Elhana and Visi left their tasks and came bearing food, dodging streams of carts loaded with barrels of pitch sap, and later provisions of dried and packed fruits, vegetables, grains, raisins, apricots, apples, rice, beans, flour, and salt. And finally puncheons of wine.

In the evenings we pushed barrows of waste and scrap. The grass was worn in every direction. Crossing and winding, trails of bare earth disappeared over hills and reappeared as threads in the distance. The Effort was suspended like a swelling wooden locust at the center of a great web of roads and footpaths.

I watched the wealth that would have been divided three ways divided a thousand. As I write this the question comes–what would I have done with my portion of the birthright? I ask in return–how am I to imagine a life without the waters and the curse of all they brought? How am I to form a vision other than that of a stunted empire of worry and want?

To conceive–in any detail–of a life beyond the one lived requires an imagination far surpassing my own.

Shem/Visi I Japheth/Elhana I **Ham**/Paan

Gather by their kind one pair each of unclean animal, male and female, and seven pairs of clean. Gather as well seven pairs of each bird.

This last instruction came. The strangest yet. We listened, then questioned. We made our attempts to decipher and, if possible, understand.

Japheth: *Unclean? Clean? Does clean mean not dirty? While it seems it should, I don't know.*

Visi: *The swine is fond of mud.*

Elhana: *What of the creatures that burrow? Is it not in their very nature to do so?*

Shem: *Fishes. Surely these are clean. No. I see my error, now that I've said it. Never mind.*

We spent from dawn to midday questioning him as he tried to teach us which was which. Part of me engaged with this chatter of labels; most of me worried after Paan. She wasn't only silent. She wasn't present. She remained unwilling to be a part of the Effort. Each evening I told her the events of the day. I feared telling her this would cause her to leave me altogether.

At last, he held up his hands, palms out, silencing us.

Father: *Only some are worthy of sacrifice to The Maker.*

Mother: *Why? Didn't The Maker give them all life?*

Father: *Of course! Clean or unclean is in the creature's habits as well as their design.*

It was at this point I turned my attention away from this boggling conversation as well as Paan's pale state to question the health of his mind.

We'd helped him build and stock a massive water chest surrounded by a forty-day and forty-night walk in any direction of sand, grass, and rock. Now we were quibbling over the eating habits, hooves, and skins of beasts? This was now his concern? From the invention of the cubit to which beast chews its cud?

Shem/Visi | Japheth/Elhana | **Ham**/Paan

Later when we were alone, we wondered what worm was feasting on his brain.

Maybe a pair of worms, said Visi.

I tossed my head back in laughter. Shem glared at her.

Her smile fled. She looked at the ground.

At dawn the village and lowlands were overrun. No one came out of their homes. People gathered on their roofs to look down on the beasts. Children leapt up and down with delight as they pointed, imitating calls and bellows. Once the animals moved out and across the valley, up toward the Effort, the streets were strewn with dung.

No one was happy with that.

Stinking steam rose in the morning sunlight. It was then I realized my primary tools in the days afloat, should such days arrive, would be a sack and a scoop.

He stood atop the lone remaining lattice presiding over the parade of creatures, his cloak lifted, filled by the breeze, his staff polished and glinting in the sun. His beard combed, oiled, and braided–his face carried a weathered beauty.

As I watched, the thought came over me. I should have been up there with him in his glory. His blood flowed in me. This moment was not solely his, it was ours. It was mine as well.

Over the days that followed, seven of them before the rains came, we camped outside, beside the Effort, under a blazing sun and clear night sky. The stars mocked him. Each breaking sunrise was an insult. I was humored at the joke. These pitched boards, begging for a sea, sat in the dirt heated by the sun and cooled by the moon. This craft built to split water, split only a growing headwind.

But the eighth day came.

Clouds descended in the night and hung low over us, swirling, brushing the top of the Effort. My brothers and I ate our dawn meal, boiled beets and quail eggs, around one of the fire pits. (Later, as the waves passed under us, our stomachs would turn in on themselves. That last meal would lay in the straw at our feet.)

As we finished eating, a drop of rain popped and hissed as it hit the embers. We leaned forward and watched the fire. Unsure. Another drop hit and snapped. Thunder broke and filled the air.

Rain.

My brothers jumped up, tossed their near-empty platters to the ground, and ran toward the ramp. I followed them, close behind. But at the last moment I passed the ramp--and ran toward home.

W

Shem/Visi I Japheth/Elhana I **Ham**/Paan

Paan, Wife of Ham

It is true what Ham says. I wouldn't have returned to this place. Ever. We made this visit for Naamah, to ease her pain. And, since we were here, I was drawn to look at his dying. To see it for myself. To see him at his long-awaited end.

I stood at the flap of his tent. It took all my will to pull it back. As I bent to look, stagnant air seeped out around me, and on it the odors that rise from an old and failing body. I did not step in to see the dying man. His words--his barrel chest and bearded booming bark--had long ago seared any feelings I had for him. When I looked in, he lay silent. Soon he would be silenced forever.

I dropped the flap of his tent and walked away.

Would that he had been silent that morning now long past. Would that he had stopped after simply calling my son's name--not gone on to curse him, Canaan, my firstborn, who went running toward him when he heard his name. Then stopped, silent himself.

But first.

One evening long before all of this.

Ham didn't speak when he returned home from the day working on the Effort.

This was unlike him. He always had a report, a plan, a comment, a matter on which he'd been thinking. He'd report the day's events whether I wanted them or not. I would listen--obedient to the human desire for details of a disaster or desperation. I had never seen the site, the structure, the silliness. This was how I came to perceive the vision which had taken hold of the family--through Ham telling me of it. I refused to be part of so much toil and waste. I remained at home, a thousand paces from the pasture.

Not looking up from my weaving, I asked why he was so quiet. He did not respond. I continued weaving and asked again. He said nothing. I paused and glanced up at him. I jumped up and ran over. Lifting his hair back from his face, I cupped his head in my hands.

What happened?

His eyes closed, he mumbled through puffy, purpled lips. *I asked the wrong question. I asked for certainty instead of faith.*

Ham was bringing home too much. The Effort was changing us from the outside in. It was altering us in ways we could see and in many we couldn't. It was raising scabs and forming scars.

I looked into Ham's eyes and began to cry. He pulled me close. Against my skin, cracked and calloused from labor, his hands felt like they had grown a sheath of bark.

Shem/Visi I Japheth/Elhana I Ham/**Paan**

I would have no part in the Effort. I'd heard the prophecy. I'd heard Noah speak over the crowds. His words did not sound like *light in the darkness*, as Shem put it, but a madman granted a solo in a chorus of evil.

I could not conceive of a prophet-father who sought to strike doubt out of his son or sacrificed generations of wealth on a boat atop a high desert.

Some mornings, as I pulled weeds from our garden, I looked out to the east. On the horizon I could see smoke from the fires at the site where Ham said our future was being built. I made no comment at his use of "our." Most mornings I didn't turn to look and the smoke rose without me.

What I did watch was the road. Quiet except at harvest or festival, there passed a constant flow of tradesmen traveling to and from the Effort. I saw them lumbering as they went and I saw their light step as they returned. Their weight of cargo turned to treasure. I did not know all of the family's wealth but with day-upon-day of such trade, I wondered at its limits.

I was glad when I saw one wagon return, its load still in place, a servant boy driving the oxen, the tradesman himself slumped in a heap with the cargo.

Shem/Visi | Japheth/Elhana | Ham/**Paan**

I thought of walking, of going and peeking at the Effort. Walking until I reached the highest knoll and dropping to my belly in the tall grass, unseen, pulling myself along on my elbows until the Effort rose into view.

Would the sight of it provide what I needed to trust, to believe? Or would it siphon what little hope and strength I had left?

w

Shem/Visi | Japheth/Elhana | Ham/**Paan**

Most evenings the women returned home. Some evenings the men did. Noah never. Shem spoke of how they were doing a great service for all mankind, *preserving the race of men*. Ham agreed, but I knew this was his lust speaking, his lust to be Noah's heir to an imagined throne in some flood-soaked land.

I spoke of my unwillingness and my concern, to each of them. Separately.

Each except Noah.

I told Shem. He listened and looked at me, without expression and without words, treating me as the heathen I suppose I was.

I told Japheth. He told me if I saw the Effort just once such thoughts would vanish like haze under a rising sun.

As they rubbed oil on their stings, I again spoke with Visi, Elhana, and Naamah.

Visi listened and nodded, but her words betrayed her nods as she told me there was a loft for me aboard the craft and she was certain I'd use it.

Elhana asked me to repeat my concerns. After a long pause she said we all bear the burden of the Effort and I was not excused.

Naamah said yes, acceptance of what was happening wasn't possible. But acceptance wasn't the goal, rather finding our place in it.

I missed working alongside them and felt, even in my refusal to join them, I was missing out. As if I'd lost them to the Effort as well.

I told Ham twice.

The first time he tried to argue with me. He spoke of the honor of being a part of such a moment ... how a new mankind would come of our clan ... how we would rule in the new creation.

The second time I told Ham to shut up his lusts and listen to me, to my words. He did, and I was content he heard me.

And with this I went silent. Words could hold no more of it.

W

Shem/Visi I Japheth/Elhana I Ham/**Paan**

I spent an entire day and most of a second watching a parade of creatures walk the crest of the hill from the west to the east. Animals I'd never seen passed by, raising dust into the morning sun, silhouetted against the horizon, dark forms in the moonlight. Ham had told me to watch for them. It unnerved me to see them obeying, behaving in accord with this madness.

    The night following, no one returned home.

    Thoughts of running away consumed me. Of leaving Ham and his family, of leaving and returning to my birth home. The thought of being held by my aged mother, of holding the hand of my sister. I knew no other man would ever have me. I would always be "that one escaped from Noah's clan."

    But staying—the Effort looming just out of sight, demanding a belief, a trust, a power of will I found both foreign and bitter.

The season before the rain, Ham told me we had nothing precious left, nothing of value to anyone. We had nothing left to trade. We were the poor. Even the pasture on which the Effort stood had been sold in trade. Noah had sold all but the tools they'd used and those items from the house Naamah demanded be kept. The family home sat unused, Visi and Shem's part unfinished, weathered, rotting.

I could not accept the Effort, but all else was being dealt away.

Should I leave? Walk away, return to my family's village? If I remained, wouldn't we soon be homeless? Four pairs of humans in a great storehouse of wood?

But what if the purpose for which the Effort was built became its purpose indeed?

Shem/Visi I Japheth/Elhana I Ham/**Paan**

A dawn came when there was no sun. I rose late in the morning to a strange, pale light. I stepped outside and looked up at a sky unlike any I'd ever seen. Day had not come, instead a colorless dusk hung in its place, clouds like bundles of muddy wool tumbled and rolled overhead. There were no animals passing. The road lay empty.

Thunder, a wave of invisible rolling granite, came across and over me. I crouched and shivered in the grass, my hands over my ears. Was it a noise from the pasture?

I jumped up and ran back into the house and locked the door. The thoughts of running away galloped in my head. I felt a new panic rise.

Again, thunder.

I did not hear Ham pounding at the door. I didn't know he was there until he took me by the arm and pulled me from the floor. We passed through the door, splintered from its hinges, and ran from the house, under flashes of lightning and amidst thunder that seemed to infuse the ground with movement.

As we ran toward it, I saw the Effort for the first time. Its ramp like a gaping, open jaw. I was seized by the size of the craft. I couldn't recall what I'd imagined, but I knew I'd failed.

What bounced in my vision as we ran was what the decades had wrought, what had come to be under the morning smoke I'd watched from our garden. Surely there could never be water enough to lift such a towering box. I looked over my shoulder and saw the curtain of rain chasing us and questioned such certainty.

As we neared the ramp, our chests heaving, I saw a great crowd converging, moving toward the Effort. The rain had already caught them and had slowed them.

And I saw—a guilty relief—we'd be able to easily outrun them.

Shem/Visi I Japheth/Elhana I Ham/**Paan**

Naamah, Wife of Noah

But for Paan, I watched each of them go in to speak with him. I hovered outside the tent. I heard strains of conversation and stretches of silence. I hovered as I cooked, mended, did all that falls to a woman to do, especially when her husband is dying. Not the least of which is to know, in detail, what is happening in her own family.

I watched them leave. I saw the looks on their faces, the pace of their steps. And after this listening and looking I will now offer my words, the words of the woman who shared her bed with Noah. A claim not meager, not meager at all.

We were children the first time I saw Noah. He came with his father to our bakery to buy bread. He didn't complain as his father handed him the loaves to put in his basket. Noah rested his chin against each loaf and breathed in its aroma. I heard him tell his father he wasn't carrying bread, he was bearing gifts from The Maker. As he lifted the basket onto his back, Noah urged his father to take a loaf and give it to the beggar who sat outside our bakery door.

As they left, I blushed at Noah's headful of dark curls. His handsome boyhood drew me in. His wise confidence set him apart from all other boys. And his face--his face carried purpose. Years yet unspooled.

In our youth, Noah and I would travel far into the wilderness, lie under the stars, and speak to The Maker. The three of us. Together.

While I believed we were heard—for I stood in the shadow of Noah's trust—I heard only silence. We uttered words of gratitude and asked for protection against the evil rising roundabout us. Noah bowed, his face against the earth, his prayer for protection reformed into a prayer for rescue.

Yes, we asked for rescue. We asked this not knowing for what we asked, ignorant of how such requests are granted.

Our sons were born—three boys in six years. A fourth dropped out of me in the eighth year—one without breath. I could count every toe. I could nearly see through his thin leaves of eyelid.

Our sons came to delight in lying with us as we basked in the moonlight, their small hands probing the expanse, reaching up as if to grasp one of the distant twinkling sparks. Leaning on one elbow, Noah told them the story passed down to him. How The Maker formed each star, how He'd hung them with care in the spot He'd prepared for them, while others He joyfully flung into the void, arcs of fiery white light streaming as they crossed over and passed each other.

Though now long past, I wish again for such simple moments together, the easy coupling of youth and belief. Before the first time Noah heard and laid bare The Maker's response.

He who hung them will hide His lights. The stars will wear a shroud of clouds. Mist will cover and consume.

Later, after the boys were asleep.
You heard The Maker?
Yes.

And these were His words?
Yes.
The question—how could this be?—I left unasked.
What do they mean, these words?
The words have shape. As I listened I saw a soaking darkness, damp against my face.
You not only heard, but saw?
Yes. The words. They stamp an image on the eye.

Noah offered no more of these hearings for many, many years. This was a great relief, a gift to me. While he repeated this one as our boys grew, nothing new passed his lips.

I later learned The Maker had not stopped speaking to Noah. Noah had simply ceased repeating what he heard. He kept the words, tucked into his cloak, letting them simmer in his soul. While I didn't know this, I did know Noah wasn't mine alone. His mind, his heart, these were moving in ways that appeared to me, and to our sons, as a husband and father aloof, absorbed in an uneasy quietude. A man you don't speak to, who can't be bothered, one who's alone when with and with when alone.

And one night, under the moonlight, I saw who we'd become.

I found him awake, standing on the edge of the pasture, looking toward the horizon.

What is it, my strange, gray-headed lover? Come in and lie back down.

He lifted a finger to silence me and then moved his hand in behind his ear and bent it forward.

I pulled my wrap back up onto my shoulder and left him there, standing, listening under the stars at the edge of the distance that had come between us.

Noah/**Naamah**

In the last dozen years before the rains came, every seventh day, Noah put on his prophet's cloak and left at dawn. He traveled beyond the river and into the hills. His hope was to speak in the center of every village, to call at the walls of every city. To seek every grower, to find and convince every wheelwright, every man of skill and source, to call on every keeper of herds, whores, and secrets. He'd return at midnight blistered and worn. This was his day of rest. The next morning, under the rising sun, he'd lift his hammer and build again.

All had a chance to listen. All had a chance to believe. No man's voice was better known in the hills, the valley, or beyond the river. His words were few but spoken often. His eyes were red from loss of sleep, while the limits of his voice were unknown. This was my Noah. He would have traveled in a circuit, giving command over the raising of a hundred water chests to carry a hundred cities.

But one held all we were.

The preparation devoured our energies and swallowed our days. I created work for my women, giving direction as if each step was part of a plan. They need not know the only sources were what I saw happening around us and my imagination. I hid my uncertainty. I tucked it away where they wouldn't see it. I worried it with my calloused fingertips, tended it, as I did all else.

None of us flourished under the strain of the Effort. Visi most easily found her place in our peculiar vocation. Her eyes bright in wonder, her light spirit was her advantage, applying muscle over mind, always busy.

Elhana, lifting her eyes to meet mine, needed my ear as she did the hard work of taking in and stowing all she saw. The grafting of grief, so familiar to a woman. Dark hair, tied on each side, her dark eyes made even darker.

Paan--at home, in a turmoil all her own--her eyes closed to it all. She told me her thoughts were awash in an unnamed, pending dread, sleep her only solace.

I sought to become a mother to these women, our son's wives. These women who had found their way, had stumbled into this life of strange tasks by loving my men. These women who--if the vision took shape--would be the mothers of all living.

The distance that had come between Noah and me revealed itself unannounced, like a specter that passes through the corner of a room, a reminder all is not well. Shem asked Noah how we would gather the animals. It was a simple question, one seeking instruction not revelation.

Noah made a wide circle with his arm, as if rounding up the hills, valley, the rock-strewn horizon and gathering it to himself. The gesture ended with his hand on his chest.

The creatures will come to me to be saved, just as they came to Adam to be named.

There it was. The edge of the distance that had come between us. I was learning to sense when this distance was approaching. While our sons were given the skills needed for raising the Effort, this was the skill I came to possess.

We were already a menagerie, a visual prophecy, a drama and declaration upon a pasture. But once the animals arrived, we became a spectacle. A new kind of wonder, the sort of which gods stop to take notice.

I would never have sought such attention.

As I scanned the hillside across the valley, I could only hope this continued to be a mass of wonder-seekers and didn't become, one day, an assembled army.

Though I couldn't have known it then, I went to see Leah during the last moon before the first drops fell.

There was sadness in her eyes. Not sadness alone, but sadness laced with pity. Her tall, sturdy frame stooped as she looked at me. We were dear to each other. We had learned to walk, holding hands among the ovens in the bakery our fathers owned. And now...*how this man has broken you and your family, taking your sons' youth for labor, spending all you own.*

She apologized for her blunt words.

I touched her arm and shook off her apology.

She told me it was a burden for her. A burden as if it were her very own.

I nodded.

We sat together over tumblers of cider. We spent as much time in silent reflection as we did giving it words.

As I stood to leave, she came close to hug me. She stopped short and stood for a long time. Her eyes traced the lines on my face before meeting mine. She saw fear, I'm sure. But what she couldn't have seen was I was no longer afraid because of what had become of us, or of what might be our future among our people. I was afraid of what would be if Noah was right. I was afraid the waters would come.

Noah/**Naamah**

All the wellsprings of the great
deep burst

And the casements of the
heavens were opened.

G.7.11

IN THE MIDST: A Collection of Keeps

Shem, Son of Noah

In a corner of the bottom deck I paused and listened. A sound. Pounding. A muffled pounding against the wall. This was not the measured pounding of a man at work. I knew that sound well, and I was alone. There were not creatures in this part of the store hold. I stood still, a single candle in hand. I stood at the wall, then crouched, my palm flat against it. I listened. It came again. Jerking my hand away I realized—the pounding was coming from the other side, the outside.

I perceived the sound was that of a rock held in a fist, beating against the outside of the Effort. The pounds grew fast, like a rage, then, as the candle burned lower, grew softer like a beg. Then—a different sound—the rush of water. The craft jostled and settled. The pounding was gone.

I would never again stop on that bottom deck, in that corner, without the memory of pounding—a rock held in a fist. A message, a cry for help. And me, on the other side. On this side. Shocked. Failing to bear up even a knock of response.

Shem/Visi | Japheth/Elhana | Ham/Paan

The Effort groaned as it began to shift, to turn. I imagined our weight scraping the pasture into waves of mud. As the craft lifted free, the animals became so loud we could not speak to each other. Was this a cacophony of praise or a chorus of panic? A few hand signals allowed us to converse above the din.

I escaped to the top deck, to one of the windows. Sharp, piercing sounds cracked across the surface of the water. A sound like the splitting of rock mixed with the rumble of thunder and slapping sheets of rain. Lightning revealed creatures swimming–dogs, camels, an elephant with its keeper still riding it. People and livestock were clustered, adrift on islands of debris.

Over the next days the floats broke apart and vanished. Those riding them slipped under or were sucked under by sea beasts. In the gray light I saw such beasts surface, tentacles like the limbs of a sycamore and great arched humps stopping, reshaping the waves.

Sleep no longer regularly visited any of us. I remember Mother climbing a ladder, pulling herself up the final rungs, and stepping onto the floor next to Visi and me, a gourd of rain water sloshing in her arms. She sat down in front of a trio of candles Visi had just lit. Visi hadn't planned this, but one flame for each day Mother had been awake.

Mother bent close, peering down into the reflection of herself. She prodded her face as if inspecting an abandoned creature she'd just found. The start of a scar had formed just below the bottom lid of her eye from the claw of a sand cat. The smell of singed hair filled our loft as she muttered, *this woman's eyes have seen too much.*

Father would later say the scar under Mother's eye lent her the exotic. He was right. A flaw, acquired from living such a life, held an untold story. It begged a question. Beauty and mystery. That most desired pair.

With less allure, we all carried scars.

During the building we formed many window frames. Father held the boards across his knees and I bent over him, driving the joining pegs at each corner. On one corner he or I misjudged. I will own the error. It was my failure. I felt a strange softness in the final stroke of the hammer and saw Father jump.

I stood back, the hammer still in my hand, unsure what to do. I had driven the peg through the board and through the palm of his hand. With a grunt he tugged his hand free and wrapped it in his cloak. He did not look at me as I muttered an apology. He said nothing. From that day forward, when at rest, his hand curled like a talon.

I suffered as well. Deep into the voyage, after tending the hoofed ones, I was descending one of the ladders into the third hold. Six rungs down, the Effort rolled and dropped into the trough of a wave. I lost my balance

Shem/Visi | Japheth/Elhana | Ham/Paan

and swung wide, hanging by one arm. My watering pot fell and burst on the floor below. I struggled, trying to pull myself over onto the rungs. My legs flailed, seeking a foothold.

I woke on my back, my thick black hair matted with blood, dried stiff as an armadillo's carapace. My breath shallow, many moments passed before I was able to piece together where I was. My head throbbed. I couldn't remember why I was lying there. And I couldn't give names to the faces that hovered, asking me if I was able to get up. Their images felt to me like distant places I'd visited as a child.

Over the days that followed, their names returned to me in my sleep, in fitful sleep, like deciphering ancient shapes on cliff walls at twilight. Visi plucked fistfuls of down from the undersides of waterfowl and stuffed it inside my smock for warmth. Thus began our knowledge of the louse.

Father was lying with his eyes half open. He lifted his arms out from under the wool. Heat rose from him. I gave him water, droplets of which sat on his beard like dew on the coarse hair of a slumbering beast.

Do you remember the fire, Father?

He didn't answer.

W

We hung a gong on each floor of the Effort as a means of calling for help should there be a need—a loose animal, a leak discovered, a stowaway found in our cargo. The likelihood of each of these was far less than the one before. Each gong had a different tone, according to the floor on which it hung. We memorized these tones, but we only had one occasion to use a gong. And I was the one who struck it.

I was on the second floor, amongst the mammoths in the darkness of early morning. When in with these gentle creatures, it was as if you were in a jungle of hair. Not only was there the hair that hung in thick curtains from their sides and underbellies, but that which they shed into heaps.

This is why I didn't see the flames at first.

Out of the corner of my eye I thought I saw a flicker at the far end of the floor. I knew I had not lit a candle. I dismissed it and continued working. Then, again, I saw a burst of orange light where there shouldn't have been any. By the time I got out into the open, the flames were causing pitch to bubble and run down the wall. I spotted splatters of wax. A candle had fallen from the floor above and bounced into one of the grain holds.

I struck the gong and began to douse the flames using every pail of water I could find. I ran up and down the floor, grabbing pail after pail. I struck the gong a second time and used every piece of cloth I could rend–

Shem/Visi | Japheth/Elhana | Ham/Paan

feed sacks, waste tarps, my own cloak—to reduce the flames to embers.

In the end we'd used all the water on that floor and thrown all the water from the floor above. Having used our cloaks and under-wraps as well, my brothers and I stood soaked, covered in soot, and very nearly naked, staring at the smoldering wall, charred bin, and blackened grain scattered all around us.

Father made his way down just as we began to sweep up the loss. We looked over at him, anticipating words on a continuum between reprimand and condemnation.

There you go, he said. *Fire and water. Two elements best kept in their places.*

He turned and began to climb the ladder he'd just descended.

We turned and looked at each other, leaning on our broom handles, smoke hanging from the ceiling above us.

Do you remember the fire, Father?

His eyes still half open, his brow furrowed as if he'd forgotten something.

Did I ever thank you boys for putting out that fire?

Just as we'd built the Effort from plans not our own, it now pushed through the storm without our assist or guidance. I had to believe The Maker would not allow such a craft to be made only to be tipped into the deep.

This faith was necessary, for any sense of direction was lost. North to south, east to west; these left us as we drifted, blind to both the heavens above and the land deep below. It ceased to be clear if we were moving or bobbing in place. The sky coursed above us, the sea surged beneath us, knowing not our weight upon it.

We no longer carried more than a single flame to traverse the lower decks. We knew the alleys between each crate and cage. We knew which beasts were where, when they slept and when they woke. We knew which would bare their teeth and which would use them. We knew which had young and which ate them before we could notice. Our footsteps pushed clear the fodder and waste. Our crusted and calloused feet rubbed smooth soft ruts in the wooden planks we had laid.

One expects to be defined by his work, or the customs of his clan, or those which he marries into. Perhaps a man is known for a great feat of valor, an unhidden habit, or a fall into vice. These could, with reason, be his life's measure.

Never does he imagine his life will be defined by weather.

Shem/Visi | Japheth/Elhana | Ham/Paan

A rumor spread. During the night there had been a split in the clouds. Elhana said mother had spotted a star, a bright star hanging just above a purpling horizon.

We gathered on the top deck. We watched as dawn chased darkness. And we saw the gray shell under which we'd floated for so long had indeed cracked, the clouds had formed edges in the night. In the first light of dawn the clouds began to drift, revealing blue--a blue we'd once craved and nearly forgotten. Soon the sun lifted off the horizon and cast its light all around us. The blazing, unhindered light overwhelmed us. We closed our eyes, covered our faces, and looked at each other from between our fingers. Our shadows fell tall and slender behind us. Somewhere just below deck a bird sang--a sound I realized at that moment, I'd never heard aboard the Effort.

Day had found us again!

Father came up the ladder and stood at the edge of the Effort, his arm extended in the morning sun, one of Japheth's doves perched on his wrist and one of Japheth's ravens perched on his elbow. They spread their wings and fluttered in the mid-morning sun.

The rest of us shed our outer cloaks and bathed in the sunlight. Our hair and skin turned warm, deep breaths of sea air. The Maker had indeed remembered us. That evening, for the first time, we saw the sun set over our ocean.

Morning and evening again.

Shem/Visi I Japheth/Elhana I Ham/Paan

T he next midday the dove jumped from Father's wrist with a warble and began to circle over us in ever-widening arcs higher and higher over the Effort. I imagined what we must look like from up there, an island of wood rising and falling on the greatest ocean ever created. Our necks grew stiff. We laid down on the deck to watch. After reaching her height, the bird began her wide swoop and returned, her chest heaving, finding rest back in the crook of Father's elbow.

We watched many flights. For the dove carried our own desires to fly away, to leave behind--even for a few moments--the feeling of gopher wood against our feet. To step off into something else. Somewhere else.

And a hint came. A hint of how such desire might be met.

One evening we watched the dove descending toward us. Her circles had grown wide. We sometimes lost sight of her among the distant waves and twilight.

Is she carrying something? asked Paan, pointing.

We all stood. Japheth leaned forward. *I can't be certain. Perhaps?*

Yes, said Paan. *I can see. In her beak.*

We all began to turn with the dove in her passes over us. I tried to see the detail Paan had seen. How could she be so certain? I wondered if her recoil from the smoke and sun of laboring on the Effort had saved her eyesight.

Finally, after a last wide arc, the dove hovered and landed on Father's forearm.

There it was. A fresh olive leaf tucked in her beak. Father held open his palm and she released it.

We passed it between us. The tender green skin held a fertile beauty. We breathed deep its rich tang, a scent from both the past and future at once. What I saw in my

Shem/Visi | Japheth/Elhana | Ham/Paan

father's face was hope, a softening. The clouds moved out of his eyes and the wrinkles fell loose from his face. His eyes closed, his lashes watery wet, his cheek touched the dove's breast. Could he feel the tiny panic of her heart?

How will we know when we can leave the Effort? I asked.

When the dove doesn't return, said Father.

Within two new moons the Effort ceased to move.

Cradled in the rock of a mountain side, the Effort rose each day without moving as the water receded, pushing us skyward. Our work remained the same as we appeared to rise higher, higher, the earth dropping below and around us. We gave up guessing which day we would put our feet on the rocks that held us, which day the dove wouldn't return.

But the day came. The day came when she didn't.

W

Father came around in the early morning, each of us at work among the crates and cages. He tapped us on our shoulders, nodded in silence, and motioned for us to follow him down to the bottom hold. One-by-one we gathered and huddled together around him, still holding the tools of morning--brooms, weaving needles, pails, baking tongs. We wondered for what purpose we'd been pulled from our chores.

Mother held a fistful of candles at arm's length, casting light onto the wall of the hold. Father brushed his calloused palms over the dirt and grime, bending down, reaching up, pausing to feel the grain of the gopher. Together they moved, the light running just ahead of his searching fingertips. Maintaining our huddle, we moved with them, still unsure what it was we were witnessing.

After two passes the length of the hold, Father stopped for no reason we could riddle. He waited as mother lit a half-dozen more candles. In the yellow glow he moved yet closer to the wall, brushing it once more. In a cloud of dust he stood, silent, facing the wall. I had just parted my lips to break the silence when, with the edge of his thumbnail, Father uncovered the thin seam of the ramp.

He stepped back and lifted his hammer.

We drew a breath.

Shem/Visi | Japheth/Elhana | Ham/Paan

Visi, Wife of Shem

The sound of thunder filled our chambers like a thousand hammers clattering down the beams over our heads. As we lifted and began to drift, the sensation of being afloat for the first time caused me to fall to my knees. I grasped the base of a post and pulled my legs in under me. I felt we were being lifted, hoisted up, not only upon the rising waters but also upon the last breath of every living being.

I thought of my mother and wondered yet again where she had gone and if she thought of me in all of this.

I thought of my father and the waters rising around his neck and his feelings of being trapped, smothered–at last relating to me.

A terrible rumble sounded against the bottom of the craft. Vibrations at the soles of my feet. Was it a sea creature rising? Was it the release of souls from the depths? Shem ran to the top and looked. *Great geysers, hundreds of them all around us, in every direction,* he said. *Columns of steam pull the water up and mix with the roiling sky. Billows rise from under our craft as we drift over one spout, then another.*

Was the land churning under us like a great stew? Would the land be whole when the waters drained away? Would the waters drain away? Would we know the landscape when we saw it again? Would the earth ever again be fit to hold us? Was the Effort a chest of rescue or a box for burial? Such questions sat in the back of my throat while others passed through my lips.

We took from the bundles of candles we had made and posted them in nooks and joints throughout the craft. Our shadows shimmied up the walls and bobbed on the ceilings of the holds. Caught in the light, the eyes of the beasts glowed; frogs and insects green, reptiles red, furry and four-legged beasts yellow. The moths and winged insects which had found their way to us circled the flames. Those not snatched out of the air by flittermice often ventured too close to the heat and fell in a puff, entombed in the slow ebb of wax. Their offspring repeated the deadly fire dance a day or two later.

The soaking gray dawn and misty dusk were one. Days interrupted our nights and we lost our nights in a shuffle of days. We slept when we could no longer work and we worked when we were not asleep.

Scoop after scoop, barrow after barrow, from off the rail of the top deck we created, on the waves behind us, a trail of human and animal scrap and waste that had the appearance of a path an oxcart might traverse.

I still have a collection of keeps I picked up as I labored among the creatures. My favorites are a tiger's whisker, a tuft of mongoose fur, a crocodile scale, and the molar of an ape.

Shem/**Visi** l Japheth/Elhana l Ham/Paan

On my only other visit to Noah's tent in his last days, he sat hunched over the edge of his bed, as he did for a few minutes each afternoon, when he was able.

His shriveled legs dangled. He no longer made attempts to lift himself to his feet. His eyes were open, but could he see? One eye stared down at his feet. The other hung, half closed, cloudy and unmoving.

I stepped over and stood before the dying prophet.

I have a question never answered. Perhaps you know.

He made no response.

What is a skink? Do snakes and salamanders mate?

I recognized the question was an odd one, but he should know. He seemed not to hear my ask. I stood before him many minutes. I wondered if he knew I was still in the room. Then he spoke with near-youthful clarity.

I've seen salamanders eaten by snakes. This seems no prelude to tending each others' eggs.

This was, as Elhana once said of Noah's words, not an answer but a conclusion.

Oh, I nearly forgot. I have as well the claw of a sloth. I kept all of these items in a pouch made of grape leaves coated in pitch. I will find this, bring it here, and leave it with these writings.

The violence of the Effort striking land caused us to cry out. The craft pitched and yawed in a long, deep groan. This was followed by the sound of scraping, the entire craft vibrating as the Effort pushed onto and across the mountain rock. We had stopped. For days the waves rolled against and under us in our mooring. Lodged in place, our craft baked in the sun and shuddered in the wind.

Paan, Elhana, and I began to speak of the trek back to our home. We spoke of what we knew—the pasture, the river, the valley below—but we soon came to realize home would be wherever we had stopped. We would see another part of the world, a new part, created by water. We would be foreigners where there was no native. Home was a word we'd struggle and strive to refill with meaning.

Two days after the rain had stopped, all of us joined Noah on the top deck in the wind and soft evening light. We saw the Effort was held fast between two rocks, wedged, the rocks like a pair of teeth biting into the wood. Over the coming days, as the waters continued to recede, the Effort would shift and settle, like a great drifting log brought to a stop in the bend and shallow beyond a river's rapids.

The waterfowl that had ridden atop us were gone. Noah held Japheth's two birds, the dove and the raven, his arm extended toward the horizon. We waited as the raven looked out across the water, dialing in her beady eyes on the crest of one wave then another. She turned into the wind, stretched and rattled her wings. Finally, she pushed air into our faces and flew in a straight line away from us, her call like blurts of joy. Smaller and smaller she grew as she flew. Making a turn on the line of the horizon, she grew larger again and passed over us, her course unhindered, alone in flight. Once satisfied at the lack of

Shem/**Visi** | Japheth/Elhana | Ham/Paan

any other roost, she returned to the perch of Noah's outstretched arm. I held a few pinches of grain out to her. Her beak probed my palm, snatching one kernel at a time, then two.

We stood at the wall in the bottom hold, huddled together at the edges of a pool of candlelight. The other five were whispering, sharing their questions.

What is Noah doing, pacing the wall like a caged beast?

Why were we called down, away from our chores, to witness this?

Is there a prophecy embedded in the wood? This question took root and caused considerable chatter. *Is he divining, drawing it out from the pitch?*

I remained silent. I saw what was happening. I thought of running back to the loft to get my extra cloak.

Wind will soon swirl around us, I said, too low for anyone to hear.

Without a word or glance, Noah took a candle from Naamah, turned from the wall, and stepped between us. We watched as he went down the length of the hold and around a corner. The questions stopped. We stood in silence. A thud sounded, the lid of a box dropped shut. Here he came, moving back down the hold toward us.

He blew out the flame he had held, tossed it to the floor, and stepped back into Naamah's candlelight. Again he faced the wall, his forehead nearly against it. Then, taking a step back, he lifted his hammer to his shoulder.

Shem/**Visi** I Japheth/Elhana I Ham/Paan

Japheth, Son of Noah

I felt the craft shift and lean as it rose. I thought of home, of the river that crossed below our pasture. The river in which we waded as boys, in which I'd learned to swim, on which we'd skipped rocks. The place that held my boyhood, the banks on which I'd stood, from which I'd jumped, were now surely overflowed, softened, collapsed onto the rocky riverbed. The river--bulging, swirling with grass and straw--losing its way among the trees and hills, and finally the very flow itself being swallowed up, lost in the rising tide, in a wilderness of waves.

The earth was then welter and waste and darkness over the deep and God's breath hovering over the waters.

I remembered the words of my grandfather, given him by his grandfathers. The story they told and retold of the beginning.

And I saw it. Welter and waste. Laid out before me.

During the tenth night of rainfall Elhana and I spoke of how it would surely cease by morning. I mentioned our assumption to Ab.

He looked at us, then spoke as if revealing a secret, a certainty he'd always had, perhaps found clutched in his fist at birth.

We've only seen a start.

That night I woke from a dream, crying out, panting.

I'm alone on the Effort. I am ancient, gray-bearded, dying. I lay in the bottom hold, my joints stiff, swollen, and failing. My hands and feet are numb and layered in callouses. My hearing and eyesight, however, are faultless, surpassing those of my childhood.

The fifth and sixth generations of beasts swarm. No cage can hold their numbers. They growl and hiss for food but I have nothing and cannot pull myself to my feet. Their dung lines the walls, pushing forward in drifts all around me.

The next morning, the crust of sleep on my eyes, I came across Ab in the grain hold. He did not see or hear me. I did not approach him. He sat on the floor, a candle in his fist, his elbows resting on his knees, his chin to his chest. Sweat and murmurs before The Maker.

... save us from this floating box, this Eden we keep, this craft of our hands ... the watery expanse of Your endless ocean upon which we now drift ...

I turned and rushed up and out of the hold. Hearing such a prayer caused me to grow cold in the chest.

Did he not know more than we about what would come next?

Shem/Visi | **Japheth**/Elhana | Ham/Paan

All these years later, the details of the story told and retold, and Shem still doesn't believe me.

As he hit the gong a second time, I was standing right next to him, dowsing the flames with my cloak. He needn't have hit the gong twice. Ham was above us, throwing down water.

I cannot convince him of these simple facts. He will not abandon, nor edit, his memory of the fire.

Shem/Visi I **Japheth**/Elhana I Ham/Paan

To the naive, living in a floating chest with thousands of breeding pairs of animals may sound exotic. Exciting. Fascinating even. I tell you it is not. It is not at all. There is the sound. The stink. The constant movement of the waves under us and the creatures within.

In every corner of this craft, I see my mistakes, every missed cut and poorly hewn plank. I am reminded of the ways I have fallen short. Beyond this, I wonder what words I could have used to bring along more of the others. I spoke what I was given. Over and over, I spoke what I was given. It was all I had. It was not enough. And then I ask, what have I put my family through in all of this? Yes, they are the remnant, but what of the scars this will leave? In what ways—seen and unseen—has my clan been altered forever?

O, this task given me by my Maker. I do as I've been instructed. I follow the prophecy. I keep. I tend—even as I yearn. I yearn for a single moment alone in a hillside vineyard, leaves lifted in the evening breeze, clusters of fruit warm from the day's sunlight. I yearn for this as an old man grown lame yearns to feel once more the earth against the pads of his numb and flaccid feet.

Last summer one of my grandsons and I went back. I had not been inside the Effort since I was a much younger man. As we walked, climbed, and wandered, torches in hand, I stepped into the loft where Ab and mother had slept. I saw the chalk, still hanging, pitted with age, and the marks where he'd counted the days.

And I discovered the words above, written in Ab's scrawl upon a slate, tucked away between two timbers.

I read it aloud the last time I went to see him. At the description of the vineyard came tears. I don't know why he cried. Perhaps it was hearing from himself all those years later. Perhaps it was the crush of memory and the awareness of the future lived since. Perhaps it was more

Shem/Visi | **Japheth**/Elhana | Ham/Paan

simply the fact he had become an old man, the number of his days run short, himself grown lame. Perhaps it was all these at once.

When I finished reading, he asked me to read it again. Slower.

A boy seeking to master water.

Elhana and I woke to a dense, damp silence. We lay on our backs, fear washed over us. Every animal was still. We whispered to each other just to make and hear sound. Elhana stood at the foot of the bed and lit a candle. We looked around our loft. All was just as we'd left it the night before—clothes hung on pegs, a jar of water, a worn broom, a small bowl of dried fruit. We dressed and walked out of our loft, agreeing we should climb to the upper hold.

The others were already gathered, each clutching a candle. We were the last to join. No words were spoken, no greetings exchanged. Together we listened to the silence. Had we sunk into the depths? Had the waters ceased to carry us and instead encased us?

We filed toward the ladder to the top deck. Looking up, past the top rung, it appeared a great cloth had been draped over the Effort. The top of the ladder we'd used so often dissolved into a pale cloud.

Shem went first. One-by-one we began to climb, each helping the last up the final rungs. Atop the Effort, our candlelight lost its power and softened into a collective glow. Fog. We couldn't see four cubits up or down the deck. With just a few steps we were lost from each other. We called out, our arms extended like newly blinded men, laughter erupted. But what we did see, in the silence and fog, was the rain had ceased. By midday the fog had lifted and by late afternoon the sun had warmed the deck. This was our forty-first day aboard the Effort.

Shem/Visi | **Japheth**/Elhana | Ham/Paan

My daily routine changed as I added the task of standing on the deck and watching my birds take flight in the search for land. Each day I watched my raven fly to the horizon and back. Others sometimes paused their work to watch as well. In all directions the raven passed over us, alone in the sky. Every seven days Ab released my dove to circle over us. We cast lots, guessing which day one of the birds would find land. And we cast lots again as the day of our guess passed.

Yet one afternoon, after my dove had taken flight, her warble ceased. We had seen her complete her arc but when we turned to see her come around again, she was gone. Ab and I watched for her familiar form. We scanned the sky. I called the others. *The dove has disappeared! Come, watch with us!* We all waited. We waited through sundown for the dove to return to Ab's outstretched arm. Each moment we stood under the stars fed our hope the dove was gone. And under full moonlight, with a chatter of anticipation, we gave up our watch.

I went to bed, both sad at losing her and hopeful for what her absence meant. Sleep came and I dreamt of her prying twigs from the mud and hoisting them into a new olive tree—the crown of her nest, the ivory sheen of her clutch.

Elhana, Wife of Japheth

W

The earth was flooding. Undefended, it was being overcome by a siege of waves. The Effort started to lift, to shift, to lean. I slipped open a window in the top and heard a man's voice somewhere below echoing up the wall of the craft. Again he cried out. He was cold. He could no longer feel his legs. Opening the window further I climbed up on a crate and leaned out. Rain stung my face. It was much, much colder than I'd imagined.

Shielding my eyes, I looked out into the last gray light of dusk. I couldn't see the man I had heard, but I saw he was one of thousands. Scanning over them, my wide eyes were drawn to a woman surrounded by a huddle of men. They had a catapult on a knoll, its wheels submerged in mud. The woman was bent down, laying a small bundle in the sling. I held my hand to my mouth.

With the help of the men, she was attempting to hurl a baby onto our uppermost deck.

Up, into the rain, the infant rose. Its form against the dome of the storm was like a loaf of bread wrapped in linen. It hung for a moment, exposed bright white by a flash of lightning. It then began to drop, a corner of its wrap unraveling, fluttering. Down it fell, well short of the Effort, into the mass of people gathered and rioting, chest deep in a rising slurry of grass, drowned animals, pottery, food, and scraps of wood.

I looked back toward the sling, searching for the men, the woman--a mother perhaps--her arms raised, screaming in desperation. I began to sob. The sling was already on its side, waves crashed over the knoll, the huddle of men and the woman were gone.

I've read what I've written and I shiver. Such a memory to carry. Such a memory to lay down.
I've never told anyone this.
Now I've told everyone.

We helped Paan as she caught up to all we'd been through. She was shocked at the Effort, this box of stables and souls. Visi and I had spent decades labeling and relabeling what it would mean to see our past lives washed away. Paan did this work at once.

Huddled close, nose-to-ear in the darkness those first few nights, the three of us whispered to each other. There was no reason for this hush but our angst at what was ending on the other side of the great curved wall--and what was beginning on this side.

We cried. We comforted. We cried again.

We had married these men, these sons of Noah. But how could we have known? How could we have known we would be gathered into this floating Eden? How could we have known we would leave forever the mothers on whose knees we had sat, the brothers and sisters whose hands we had held? How could we have known we would be the only orphans on earth?

For two nights I walked the lower deck alone and came again to where the ramp stood shut. The first night I found only a seam where it fit, a thin score in the wood.

The next night I searched for the seam I had found. So much had been broken in the tide on the other side, but this side of the craft appeared to be smoothed, wholly healed.

Shem/Visi l Japheth/**Elhana** l Ham/Paan

In an effort to bring us solace, Japheth picked up his reed pipe once again. I hadn't known he still had it, and certainly not that he had brought it with him.

When we were young, I first heard Japheth before I saw him. At a wool harvest feast I heard a beautiful melody coming from within a huddle of shepherds. When it ended, they clapped and dispersed. There he was, tall, lanky, smiling, a lamb asleep at his feet.

Aboard the Effort such music was a salve to the senses, like a daybreak breeze or the aroma of fresh cut wheat.

And I wondered, what similes, what metaphors for contentment would come from a future world? What healing would our wounds bring? How many years lie between us and then? Like this I began to sculpt hope from my grief.

J apheth and I awoke to a lack of sound. To the simple fact the rain had stopped.

It is true. The ceasing of a sound can frighten as much as the arrival of one.

W

Under the clear sky, on the top deck, we began to adjust to the vast space hidden from us for so long. To again see the unhindered distance between horizons brought a new crush of anxiety. Back inside, the walls and corners of the Effort brought comfort.

The calm of being contained.

Islands that hadn't been on the horizon one day, appeared the next. Over the days that followed, the earth began to swallow the waters. With this, a new force of the deep was unleashed. Great waves came, one after another, walls of water against the side of the Effort. Water piled up, rushed at, and crashed against us in rhythm—the space between these assaults just long enough to cede the question if each was the last.

Japheth sang a psalm he'd written, a lament, a prayer. A hope The Maker could hear a son of Noah.

We stand on feet for gripping rock,
Not fins, not gills, but lungs.
Bring us to land again, O Maker.
For forest we ask, for field, for home.

I was indeed rescued twice. Once from being sold, from being bought. Once from the tide, from the undertow.

    Under the tradesman's eyes, my arms lashed together, I was shoved toward his wagon.
    Before he touched me, I could feel his fingers gathering the hem of my cloak. Before he could touch me, the ropes were cut from my wrists.

    And again.

    Under a clear blue sky, up a ramp. A trail of beasts, I, among this clan of eight.
    Before being caught in the flow, drug along the underside of this craft. Before the choking, a throat full of rain--one of three women, I was lifted out.

    Why two rescues for me and none for the many?
    Why does this Maker, of whom Noah speaks, care so for me?

W

Shem/Visi I Japheth/**Elhana** I Ham/Paan

Ham, Son of Noah

The fire. I see the others have written about the fire. Yes. I remember it well.

Shem can drive a flock by starlight, broker a trade in goods or chattels, and revive memories to craft a story better than the experience once had. He has many skills, but among these is not fighting flame.

When at risk of life and limb, Shem's panic smothers his wit. He loses all ability to cooperate. When in a desperate situation he speaks in half-phrases and cannot give orders. Such events overwhelm him.

I write this not to puff myself up but to put a button on the fact. But for me and my skill of bringing a moment into submission, the Effort would have been a charred float by daybreak, a menagerie of carnage, a final disaster witnessed only by the eye of The Maker.

At the far end of the top deck, beneath the stars and moon, upon a pallet and under cover of wool, I knew Paan. Rolling on the waves, we spent a night alone together and sought to find again who we were in all that had happened—she, in her desire to ignore the Effort until the heavens fell, and I, in my advancing desire for honor among this clan.

I cradled her head in the crook of my elbow and looked for the light in her eyes. The glow that had drawn me to her when I first spotted her in the village market so long ago. Her father's linens laid out on the table between us, she said her name. It rang like a chime—confident, clear—igniting a desire within me.

But now. Her words had grown rare. Her sentences simple. Her voice a murmur.

Riding the Effort under the night sky, leaning over her, I searched for that light in her eyes. And I saw it—the shadow of it. The glow had not gone out. Together we fanned the embers, together we revived it.

And soon our hope for land grew greater, to make a home before our first was born.

Shem/Visi | Japheth/Elhana | **Ham**/Paan

Japheth's raven, Japheth's dove. I have written his name twice. I won't a third.

He was a strange boy. And never quite a man. Always looking half his age, his fair face never achieving a beard, his hair like the first wool of a lamb, his voice—always looking for a drop.

And the birds. Strange for a man to keep birds, is it not? So much cooing and coddling and combing of feathers. To keep birds and to write poetry? To sing verse?

Yet, even I must admit these birds had a purpose proven at last. I joined the others on the top deck and watched their flight. Would either bird find land? Which would do so first? We cast lots. I announced the loser would scoop behind the rhino.

Shem/Visi | Japheth/Elhana | **Ham**/Paan

As our future loomed, there was only one certainty. It would not be as we imagined.

W

Shem/Visi I Japheth/Elhana I **Ham**/Paan

Paan, Wife of Ham

Would others find a way to survive? Perhaps a pair or few would find a scrap of the Effort and float, higher and higher, finding their way along behind us. Might such scraps hold a residue of salvation?

Was it wrong to carry such hope for those who hadn't believed?

I confess I did.

For was I not one, until the last moment?

Visi first saw the marks on my body.

She asked me. Was I in danger? Was Ham hurting me? She asked in secret. Just she and I. Her face closer to mine with each question.

I asked what she meant. What marks?

She pointed. Was I not tender there?

And then I saw.

My arm was bruised where Ham had grabbed me and pulled me from the floor. My skin was purple along the backs of my thighs from where he'd lifted me and carried me up the ramp.

These are marks of rescue, I told her.

And I didn't want them to fade.

Shem/Visi | Japheth/Elhana | Ham/**Paan**

Elhana told me what she heard and saw from the top--the man's voice, the woman, the baby. She told me she'd written it. And this gave no relief.

Listening to her. Watching her tell me this. Her tears as she repeated it, trying in vain to lay down such weight.

I could only think--what if I'd run away? What if I'd left?

W

Our lives were paused as the world came to an end and began again. While the time before lays clear in my memory, the time aboard the Effort lies not in memories but in wisps of the senses. The animals with their sudden hops and jumps--wholly unpredictable movement, noise, and stench.

This was nowhere I wished to be. Not with Ham. Not with anyone. Yet, the Effort was a keeper of life. The keeper of life. The hum of life vibrated in its boards. It was a hive made with human hands, a structure I'd never have imagined--not with ten thousand of Ham's reports of its raising.

Once pregnant I came to see myself as a keeper as well. The Effort carried life. I carried life. A tiny sea churned inside me, a new one of us afloat upon it.

Shem/Visi I Japheth/Elhana I Ham/**Paan**

If I had been of no help in the making of the craft, I was of less help in the days aboard it. Between the rocking of the sea under us and the pressure of the sea within me, I lost more food than I kept. I could eat the bread Naamah made, but little else.

Ham carried me up to the deck to see the birds take their flight. Watching them turn and fly over the vast expanse of waves caused me to vomit onto the hump of my belly as I held the olive leaf. I was being cursed by the gods for my lack of belief. And this was only the start.

Naamah, Wife of Noah

Noah was the last to step down and join us in the hold. I held a single flame as we stood, huddled together, our sons and their wives, the shock and rush of having at last been driven aboard stamped upon our faces.

And in the candlelight, I heard a drop of water, then another.

My husband clutched his cloak, his fist bunched tight, his knuckles white. I looked down and saw his hem soaked and dripping, the start of a puddle had formed on the board at his feet.

This was not a journey of exploration, but a divine removal, an erasure to which only we were offered witness.

It was one matter to come and go each day. To work and return home. To leave the craft each evening—our prophesied, some-day-perhaps future—there on the pasture casting its moonlit shadow. It was what defined our work, but not our lives. Not wholly.

It was another altogether to live inside, to spend each day and each night stowed in the great cask, to make it our home, this shell of wood and pitch. As Ham said, *the longest shadow on earth was cast by the work of our hands, until the only shadow on earth was cast by the work of our hands.*

Noah had not built for himself. Not according to a whim or his own desire. I know the man. His imagination would have fallen far short of such a wonder. He built in response to The Maker. He built for us a box of salvation.

Yet, as the rains beat against the sides of our craft, I sought to reform my belief anew each time he said *The Maker is mindful of us. The waters do not wash clean His memory.*

This was not an adventure, but a holy exile.

W

Noah/**Naamah**

On a stone I made bread each day—oat flour, palmsful of rainwater, crushed salt, and a pinch from the yeast jar. Elhana and Visi would knead a loaf for each of us.

Against the dome of the storm, a loaf of bread wrapped in linen, said Elhana, the past filling her eyes. I pulled her close and gave her the first loaf.

As I handed Noah his loaf I was taken back to the more distant past, to my childhood. He rested his chin against the loaf and breathed in its aroma. He whispered a prayer. Still now, in the midst of all this, his gratitude for simple bread.

We tore and dipped each piece in warm goat's milk.

A tether to what made us human.

A block of chalk hung by a strand of hemp twine from the ceiling of our loft. On the wall Noah marked a hash for every day inside the Effort. The marks stretched down one wall, into and out of a corner and onto the next.

    As the day's last candle burned, I laid awake, my head on his chest. To the rhythm and drone of his snore I counted the hashes and wondered how many more were in that block of chalk.

Noah/**Naamah**

How often would we leap into the future if we could?
The dove was a winged prophet. With the promise of an infant and now a fresh olive leaf, behind my closed eyes a new vision began to form.

Dry ground at my feet. A dozen children dance around me, calling my name, tugging at my cloak. Singing. Laughter. A breeze in the shade under a mid-day sun.

And the waters receded from the
earth little by little,
and the waters ebbed.

G.8.3

AFTER: The Art of Holding Sway

Shem, Son of Noah

In a rush of air and light, the largest animals split the ramp's timbers and nearly broke the entry from its pegs and hinge. They fled from the Effort, down the mountainside, and onto the sunlit, bare, tide-formed earth.

Japheth, Ham, and I walked every aisle, unpinned every cage, unlatched every crate. From the top hold we could feel the draw of air each creature followed until they found sunlight. With each lift of a hook, each pull of a knob, we both gave the creatures their freedom and granted our own.

The Effort empty of life, we stood at the top of the ramp. We looked down and across a landscape that shared little with the one we had known. A lakeshore stretched as far as we could see. Beside it sat a bare plain, and beyond this rose the foothills that led to the rocky heights on which we had come to rest.

The water had left scars on the land: dry earthen swells and crests formed by the heft and shift of the sea. Rises and craters pocked a landscape, wild, unkept, waiting to be tended. All undergrowth had been washed away leaving forests of trees, arched and bowed, twisted, stripped of their leaves by the currents that had risen and rushed over them. Littered throughout, wedged in broken boughs were bony carcasses—animal, human, often side-by-side—the reins of a horse or a treasured possession still clinched in a fist, even as water-swollen flesh shrank and dried in the hot sun.

Shem/Visi | Japheth/Elhana | Ham/Paan

We dug pits and filled them with animal remains as we cleared the land. Our arrival was soon evidenced by a landscape dotted with burial mounds capped in rock.

We formed pyres of fallen trees along the foothills of Ararat. Smoke rose into the sunset night after night. The remains of those we'd never known had drifted in the open waters and settled here. We had done the same. In this way we were entrusted with the bones of strangers.

Shem/Visi l Japheth/Elhana l Ham/Paan

W

The land offered little food at first. Many animals returned to eat the last of what we had brought. Our care for them was not yet over. We tossed bales of damp and mildewed grass from the hold of the Effort. These scattered, dropped seed, dried, and were eaten. We swept and shoveled each hold of any loose grain and tossed this out to them as well. The foothills surrounding the Effort turned into the first grazing pasture, while the four-footed scavengers returned again and again to wander through the craft, seeking overlooked scraps.

The first sprouts that broke through the soil were eaten by beasts as soon as the sun warmed their stalks. We began to cut the land into grazing pastures, to hem in our fields and gardens. We built dry stone fences. We dug ditches to move water from the lake inward. In this way we formed herd ponds and a village pool.

We spent days plotting the land along the edge of the lake. Looking across the vast plain, down the lakeshore toward the horizon, I found myself expecting to see others--other survivors. But each time, as if waking, I realized there were no others.

We were mankind.

I paused to drive a stake into the ground every thousand paces. I heard nothing as I walked. Silence. No creature bellowed or called. None of the common sounds made by people gathered and working, living in a place. Only the wind in my ears and the soft break of the shore. A discomfort, an unease crept into this silence. To fill it, I spoke aloud to myself and to The Maker. Often to both. I offered to The Maker what I said to myself, but built up into the forms of question and concession--or an untidy mix of the two.

Shem/Visi | Japheth/Elhana | Ham/Paan

Clean, unclean. The confusion now clear, Father built an altar. As he worked, no distant herdsmen blew their horns. No wagons or carts passed along a roadway. No dogs barked. That world had ended. Ours was the world after the end of the world. The only sounds were Father's—the crack of stacking rocks, the soft snort of a heifer pulling against her rope of hemp, the anxious clatter of goat hooves, the snap of tinder and split of wood. And then the hollow pop of flames lashed by the wind.

Solitary sounds of worship.

The flames rose higher and grew hotter. A rivulet of blood and fat ran from the base of the altar, whole offerings split open and rolled into the fire, birds wrung, tossed in and lifted by the flames.

Father finished and turned to us, sweaty, bare-chested, his eyebrows and beard curled, twisted, singed. Visions of The Maker danced in his reddened eyes.

The next morning there was a black and holy scar upon the earth.

Shem/Visi | Japheth/Elhana | Ham/Paan

Father again received words from The Maker. We fell into an old anxiety, a familiar dread. We asked between ourselves what more could there be? We gathered to watch Father build a lattice and begin to carve words into the timbers on the side of the Effort.

Be fruitful and multiply, swarm through the earth, and hold sway over it.

With this began The Law of Noah, as it would come to be known. Japheth held a torch at the end of a pole as Father chiseled through the night.

But flesh with its lifeblood still in it you shall not eat.

Herdsmen by sun, hunters by moon. The art of holding sway. The law brought a memory from my boyhood.

Very early one morning there came a bellow from the herds, a terrible rolling bellow from the far side of the pasture. Father roused me and my brothers and we ran out into the pre-dawn dark. Rubbing sleep from my eyes, I had visions of a wild beast or a stillborn calf and a dying mother. But we found no such thing. Instead we found nomads, a small band of followers of Cain.

One stood alone, his cloak hiked, urinating in the tall grass. The others knelt in a circle under the full moonlight, feasting. They had caught two of our cows, roped their legs and staked the ropes to the ground. When they saw us they jumped up and ran, having had their fill and wishing no contact with us.

We watched them go, and as dawn brought first light we saw the damage they had done. We thought our

Shem/Visi | Japheth/Elhana | Ham/Paan

cows were dead, but they were only nearly so. These were meat-eating nomads who didn't kill. They ate meat uncooked, warm and bleeding, sliced from the haunch of a living beast.

Men such as these sunk in the depths of the flood.

Our wives spoke of those they had known before, before becoming part of our clan. Mother spoke of Leah and what she'd seen in her face that last night. My brothers and I spoke of tradesmen we had come to know, who had sold us supplies and to whom we'd given goods or payment they would never have the lifetime to use. Father voiced no such words and didn't tarry to listen to ours.

All but he wondered if what washed up on the shore of the lake—lamps, cloaks, cooking pots—had been theirs. For years such items were belched from the depths of that watery crater. Among such items we looked for clues—a carved name, a family mark, a household god, a prized trinket in a pocket.

Shem/Visi I Japheth/Elhana I Ham/Paan

She has never been one to keep her thoughts to herself. As Mother has grown older she hasn't slowed in voicing her loss of friendships and her questions over what happened. She gives them up to any of us who will listen, any of us within reach of her concern.

As we settled the land, I remember her more than once quoting the law and the covenant.

I will not inflict such contempt again.

She'd pause, giving air again to the words from The Maker, quoted to us by Father. Then she'd release her commentary on them.

Yes. Surely once should be enough.

Her thoughts were not different than our own. Her concerns were ones any of us may have posed.

Any of us except Father.

She found little comfort in Father. Making brief appearances—a recluse ruler—he grew fat on meat and too often lost himself in the blood of the vine. Of the latter he shared only drips, tippling the barrels that remained from the Once Past.

I'll not speak of Ham and what he did. I leave that to him to confess. That is his narrative. His alone to surrender or conceal. But the day of the judgment? I remember it well.

Father stepped out of his tent and stood in the morning sunlight. We all paused our work. Japheth and I watched. We knew what had happened and waited to see if he would speak of it. Would Father question Ham? Would he call to Japheth and me to offer praise for the honor we had shown him? Father stood and looked past us toward Ararat. He then spoke with the certainty of one who reports events of the previous day. Once again he bore up a dark and bitter prophecy. But this time the recipients of the revelation were limited.

Blessed be The Maker, the God of the tribe of Shem.

The Maker enlarge the tribe of Japheth, may his generations dwell in the tents of Shem. May these know peace—the giving of their daughters between them and a land as that of Eden.

But Canaan, son of Ham—Canaan be cursed. The tribe of Canaan be servants, common servants to the tribe of Shem, lowly servants to the tribe of Japheth.

Father vanished into his tent, leaving us to unpack his words.

This was not about the weather or a set of rules by which to measure the acts of men. No. This was a vision of us.

This was a tell of who we would become.

At midday Father came out again. We watched as Mother walked up to him. She spoke close, into his ear. He pulled away from her and shook his head. He looked out at us and up into the twilight sky. He turned and went back into his tent.

Shem/Visi | Japheth/Elhana | Ham/Paan

Had she asked if there was another way to make a wrong right? Had she asked if he would like to speak to Ham or Canaan? Or, more simply, if he might like to go to the lake to bathe?

The following day I asked her. What had she said to him?

She pursed her lips, waved her hand in the air, and continued weaving.

The course was set. The ancient ruts of sin and judgment were discovered, uncovered, and traversed again. The hope of a new start, this great energy of beginning, was spent within a few generations.

I have seen it as I've grown old. Obeying the judgment, we remember how to enforce the position of the servant and the served.

Or to put it another way, mankind will have to wait for another rescue. Another hope will have to rise.

The heel-crushed head, as Lemech once said, *lay somewhere before us.*

Shem/Visi | Japheth/Elhana | Ham/Paan

I'll never forget the day I met my first stranger. The first time after the waters that I couldn't guess my descendants by sight.

I was in the market late one morning and had paused in a patch of shade to eat some yogurt. As I watched the crowd flow by, I saw a common sight: a servant boy hunched under the burden of a crate of fruit with a sack of grain strapped to his shoulders. His walk was slow, paced, and purposeful. This was a chore he knew well.

A few paces behind him came a young man, dressed in colorful linen, carrying nothing but the rings on his fingers. As the pair came near, the young man lifted a piece of citrus from the crate on the boy's back and began to peel its rind. Taking a few more steps, the young man whistled. Without turning, the boy found his way to the edge of the busy street where he knelt on one knee to rest. The crate, sack, and sun remained on his back. The young man paused next to me in the shade, eating his fruit.

Letting a moment pass, then another, I turned to the young man.

From which of Noah's sons are you?

He looked over, perhaps noticing me for the first time, then back to his fruit.

Why do you ask, old man? Why should it matter to you?
I make conversation, friend. That is all.

He tossed a strip of rind onto the ground and sucked juice from the exposed pulp.

I am of Shem, if you must know. Of which son are you descended?

At first I was without words. But in my pause I found an opportunity.

I would tell our story once more.

I am Shem. Noah was my father.

Shem/Visi | Japheth/Elhana | Ham/Paan

Visi, Wife of Shem

I cried as I watched the animals descend the ramp and vanish into the wilderness. Never again would so many creatures be amassed, observed so closely, cared for as we had done. I whispered their names as they left—for a few the names of their kind, for most the names I had given as we tended and kept them.

We too descended. I turned to look. The Effort appeared small, tucked high into a nook in the mountain. I paused, pointed, and told Elhana the events that led to its stowing would be told and retold. We'd repeat them to each other and to our grandchildren as they held the hands of their own children. And our telling of it would sound like the drippings of a mad imagination.

And so it is. We tell it because it is ours to tell. And our telling does indeed sound mad, but no imagination could conjure this truth.

The first night off the craft several of us awoke in the wind, under the bowl of stars, and went back.

We wove between the broken trees, limbs trembling in the gusts. We ascended the moonlit rock, the battered ramp, and found our way into the hold. We slept in the still, stale air with its familiar odors of pitch, sour grain, and dung.

None of us had ever cleared land, laid open a field from virgin earth. We piled rocks without count, forming a jetty into the lake, the end of which would in time serve several small boats for fishing—offspring of the Effort.

We planted seeds of simple fast-growing plants like leek, cabbage, and eggplant. Within part of a season the rich loam pushed up tall grass all around us. We cut, wove, and bundled. We made roofs of dried bark planks. Our family was the only family. All builders—crafters of every kind—were gone. We attempted every skill, to make all things. What we could not make we lived without. The result was something between a crude replica of the Once Past and a rough draft of the future.

We made structure for our days. We re-created routines that did not include caring for creatures. We worked with the sun. We rested with the moon. We bathed every seventh evening in the brackish lake using soap we made from water, wood ash, boiled lamb's urine, and peppermint. The wind and the setting sun dried our hair.

Shem/**Visi** l Japheth/Elhana l Ham/Paan

We stood in the hot sun, our hands over our brows, sounding out the words. Guessing as Noah chiseled. A game of riddles.

All stirring things that are alive, yours shall be for food.

We were shocked by the meaning. The killing of creatures was not new—Noah's sacrifices, slaying beasts to protect our flocks in the Once Past. But this, this idea of slaying animals for the sole purpose of eating? This was an idea none of us would have conceived. Only the law gave us such an idea.

But bit-by-bit we came to it.

We began with a happy discovery—a corner of the gaping hole left by the Effort's ramp was swelled with a beehive dripping honey. We then came to fishing; the taking of fish was an introduction to the eating of meat. We speared and ate many fish from the lake. We split them open, stuffed them with herbs and fruit. We then steamed them in shallow pits lined with embers, between layers of green grass.

In time, while tending and keeping, I learned also to read splits and joints, not for making structures of wood, but where bones are best separated. The rending and carving of flock into food—butchery was born of my delicate hand.

Shem once came up behind me, put his arms around me and said, *you have learned to wield a knife against "stirring things." When starting the world again, one learns of his wife anew.*

I came to prefer the making of meat over planting. Moving the earth came with its own troubling reveals. For a furrow could not be turned without a find—a coin, a spoon, a tooth, something more—a cache of small bones.

I remember asking Shem as I lifted them from the dirt and laid them in my palm, *is this a claw or a child's hand?*

He did not answer quickly enough.

W

We had seen the sky do much—dump water, flash with light, boil and churn, pull water up from the sea in great funnels—but great arching strips of color was a new feat.

The offspring of the Slate Donkeys stood, leaning on each other, their jaws parted, their eyes rolled up toward the colored heavens. If they could speak, what might they say?

Our clan is blessed, most blessed among all the hoofed clans of the earth. For we were chosen to bear the drawings, chosen to bear the sacred slates in service of all the beasts of the earth, in service of all mankind forevermore.

I imagined words such as these, chanted twice through as they stared up into the sky, their donkey teeth clacking at the close of each syllable.

I am compelled to speak of Ham and Paan and what came of them. She was dear to me, with her tender strong-headedness and her skill of quiet suffering. I was present for Canaan's birth.

It was a joy for us all. But her joy was short.

When Noah didn't bless Canaan I took her gifts of lamb hock and salad of squid.

Later, when the judgment was given, no gift could console.

She had gone beyond my reach.

Seeing her again, I see we are old women who don't speak of their pasts, but wear them. She is ragged. She walks as if broken at the waist. Her joints appear to be loosed by sorrow. Her face, neck, hands, elbows, knees—all I can see of her—have been pulled loose by weather, labor, and distance.

I ask about Canaan. She says he is for she and Ham a shared tumult, a son from another lifetime that feels not their own.

She is still beyond my reach.

Shem/**Visi** | Japheth/Elhana | Ham/Paan

Japheth, Son of Noah

In the beginning, as I stepped onto the soft soil at the base of the mountain, the sensation of movement was enough that I stared down, expecting to see the ground roll under my feet. For many moons I felt the rise and fall of the waves under me when I stood still or lay on my back to sleep. We all did. The waterborne memory in our bones.

We carried down seedlings we had grown in the sunlight atop the Effort, as well as the tools we'd packed in sawdust. In our hands these brought back habits and skills--bits of the Once Past began to appear as we worked. And new ways came too as we began again to become mankind.

And part of becoming mankind was to see the first birth, to hear a new cry, a new voice. The first voice of a new world.

At twilight, under the rising moon, we sat in a circle and passed Canaan among us. Each of us held him. We kissed him. We spoke to and about him. We wondered at all we'd seen and now being safe in this new place, with the promise of another generation in our arms. At last, Naamah passed his tiny frame to Ab.

Ab lifted Canaan close and studied his palm-sized countenance, a blessing forming on his lips. We watched and waited, smiling, anxious to hear words of favor, words that would tell us who this newborn man would be.

Ab moved the infant closer, his gray beard draped over Canaan's fleshy legs. Ab made a sound--the start of a word--then released his breath in a throaty sigh. His lips tight, he stared into the baby's face. At the last moment he stood, walked over, and placed the boy back in Paan's lap. He turned and stepped out of our circle, the firelight revealing only his back as he walked away, with purpose, into the night. Naamah jumped up and ran after him.

We sat and looked at each other. Paan buried her face in Ham's cloak, the child curled between them. No one uttered the question aloud. No one spoke at all.

What was it? What had held back the blessing? What had Ab seen in this little one's eyes?

Shem/Visi | **Japheth**/Elhana | Ham/Paan

When I see a few deer at the base of Ararat—which I often miss, for they blend into the brush with their bodies the color of wood and skulls that grow sticks—or some smaller creature more closely crosses my path, I do not dwell on it. I don't stop and observe in wonder as others do. Instead, I recall in what hold, on what deck, in what corner or aisle their kind was kept. I recall what we fed them, how the color of their coat changed, or how their habits were altered after months without open space or sunlight.

And how our habits were altered as well.

W

Ab had heard The Maker and was writing again. This time it was not lines and numbers on slates but demands and decrees in hardwood on the side of the Effort. Dark, pitch-covered chips bounced off the rocks below as one letter, one word at a time, the laws were revealed in light brown gopher wood.

The dread and fear of you shall be upon all beasts of the field and the fowl of the heavens, in all that crawls on the ground and in all the fish of the sea.

As I read this, I remembered the ramp falling open, the animals stampeding, running off the Effort like newly hatched ants from a toppled hill. I'd imagined, at the time, they had pent up energies and a desire for the expanse of the land. But with this I wondered anew. Had they run from us out of dread and fear?

After the laws had been written, only once more did Ab tell us the words of The Maker. The Maker who had once commanded the clouds to turn gray and cover the earth now commanded them to take shape, to form a crown of color.

With this troth I give a sign in the heavens. Though the heart of man be darkness within darkness, I will not inflict such contempt again. While the earth remains, sowing and harvest, summer and winter, sunlight and moonlight will not cease.

I have spent my life since reflecting on those words, believing, yet straining to hear them anew in each peal of thunder.

During my last visit with Ab in his final days, the quiet of the infirm rising, I remembered being in his tent once before.

Many years earlier, in the darkness before dawn, I'd come and spoken to Ab. I'd told him what Ham had done. What he had told Shem and me he had done. How he stood over Father Ab and looked, and the delight Ham had in telling it, and the light in his face. I told Ab too of Shem and me carrying the wool, our backs to him in honor.

We did not look on the shame that came of the fruit, Father Ab. We did not see what Ham saw, but instead we covered your nakedness.

As soon as I finished speaking, I saw the fire in Ab's face. He did not lift his voice. Each word came, one after the other, each word sounded of heft and heat.

I'll not have the Spirit of Cain in this place. I'll allow no residue of what was washed away.

And as he finished speaking, I worried. I worried at what I had done in coming and telling.

Ab said he would not allow, and he did not. He stepped from his tent the next day and pronounced new words, words formed to carve out and label, to declare what would come of what had been done. Words not of a father, savior, or priest, but of a judge.

At dusk, following the next harvest, Ab held a torch to the base of every vine in the vineyard. Cinders lifted on gusts at midnight, orange glitter against the starlit sky. At dawn the vineyard was a pasture of ash. In the mid-morning sun Ab came down from his tent, knelt, and scoped a palmful of ash onto his head.

We'd begun again to become mankind. We found our way to those ancient and familiar paths of mind and heart,

Shem/Visi | **Japheth**/Elhana | Ham/Paan

first carved in the brush under the tree in Eden—and kept clear by every soul since.

There in his tent again, I wanted to tell him. To let him know so he'd not be shocked. To warn him.

Ab, Ham too will be in to see you.

He did not open his eyes or offer any suggestion he'd heard me.

I leaned close and took a breath to repeat myself. I held my words as I watched a tear rise in the corner of his eye and roll, heavy and slow, into his beard.

We all carry the weight.
Years later a son of a son of Canaan's was killed. He was crushed by a tree he was felling to build a house for his overseer. A hole was dug at the spot where he died. His body was rolled into it and covered over, like a cat covers its dung.

I went and placed a pile of stones to mark the grave of my unknown, distant nephew.

Elhana, Wife of Japheth

Ham named his first son Canaan. He was born upon the rocks of Ararat. The cries Paan made as he came took on the rhythm of the waves on which he'd been conceived. Paan was the first of us to give birth and her child was the first to never know what we came to call the Once Past.

One mourns for the old woman whose end comes at last. Her death leaves a gap and closes a path to the past. One mourns a child born without breath. Such death snuffs a future only imagined. But how does one mourn the loss of everyone she has ever known? So many souls swept up and piled in the deeps?

Canaan came as a coda to so much death.

I looked out at the smoke from the pyres. I felt each breath I drew and knew it was a gift from The Maker. And I saw the others—this family, at once familiar and peculiar—for this was my tribe, our tiny huddle of humans lifted out, saved from the abyss.

Smoke from the pyres drifted up the mountain with smoke from the altar Noah built. Thanksgiving offered for us not being sacrificed on the waves in the rolling fog. We were not among the disappeared. A stunned gratitude to The Maker fell over us all. A gratitude words could not prop up.

Instead, names from the Once Past, those we had known, were exchanged between us. And not always names but phrases that belonged to faces. Their voices and words echoed in our heads, spilled from our lips.

Sometimes this brought knowing laughter, sometimes tears.

Silence always followed.

w

Shem/Visi I Japheth/**Elhana** I Ham/Paan

Under the descent of the sun we sat around the evening fire and each held Canaan—shared joy passed between us.

(If only this were it. This simple scene. One sentence. At dusk, our family gathered in the firelight.)

Why would Noah not throw his arms wide to my son?
Late that night Paan asked me this. I was silent. Questions without answers. More draff left by the receding of the deeps.

I spoke with Visi to try to form words for Paan, but Visi, with her blood-stained hands and brute ways was of no use. She brought food to Paan, first thinking Paan would want to eat, then thinking lamb and squid could mend, ease, bring comfort.

I spoke to Naamah. She said she knew this man the best. And at such a time, she knew the man the least.

In secret, women have long done what needed done.

The next moonless night I went back to Paan. I brought Visi and Naamah.

At the edge of the lake, under the night sky, we laid Canaan in the tall grasses. I put one hand upon his forehead and the other under his thigh.

A new heresy—I conjured words where there were none.

I offered a blessing.

Shem/Visi I Japheth/**Elhana** I Ham/Paan

T he Law of Noah could be seen from the base of Ararat. We stood in the morning sunlight and read the last of it.

I will requite human life. He who sheds human blood, by humans his blood shall be shed, for in the image of God He made mankind.

To kill a human was to strike at the image of The Maker and bring death upon oneself. For generations each birth was a celebration, the image anew, another life after so much death. For generations this instruction on life held in check our passions, our angers. The violence of hand and heart for which man is now known.

But like a tattoo, it faded.

Shem/Visi I Japheth/**Elhana** I Ham/Paan

The rainbow was a sign, a mark left behind, the wake of The Maker.

I've heard some demand, *Show me this God of Noah.* I need no one to show me. We carved a trough through His ocean.

Shem/Visi I Japheth/**Elhana** I Ham/Paan

Why did Noah turn to wine?
For the same reason so many do. Our past, the weight of what lies behind us, is too often what pulls, too often what defines us.

And habits follow.

w

Shem/Visi I Japheth/**Elhana** I Ham/Paan

Within a day of Noah's dark prophecy, Paan and Ham took all they had and vanished into the wilderness. They fled under the moonlight like rabbits at the scent of a wolf.

I could offer a blessing where there was none, but the judgment—I could not portend to erase, to soothe such a scald.

Ham, Son of Noah

We all have scars from the work of building the Effort. Some you see. Most you don't. Those you can't, the scars on our souls, are made visible in our actions, in what we come to sum up as one's character.

I can still feel the outline of the edge of the hammer head. The tool fell from the rafter. The granite weight of it formed a divot in the bone on the top of my foot, outlasting both weather and time.

But this lack of blessing–this was a new injury, an invisible but far more agonizing, far gorier wound. It was an injury formed by silence. No words where words should have been.

I was helpless against such weaponry. Had Methuselah still been among us I would have sought a blessing from him. I would have laid my wailing son across his ancient, bony lap. Instead, I could do nothing.

It is a frustration like none other when you've been wronged and there's no recourse to be sought.

I listened to this word buried in the Law. *Swarm*. All the earth was open to us. The lands as far as we could see—and those we could not—lay empty, awaiting us. Our generations would take hold of the entire earth and settle it in peace, unopposed. Never again would there arise conflict between or within the clans of men.

This was the depth of blatant naivety I so easily attached to such declarations.

As for *stirring things*, the first time I put meat from a land-dwelling beast in my mouth I gagged and spewed. Stringy sinews separated from bone by force. What manner of woman does such a task? My empty stomach ached for the first harvest and a warm bowl of boiled rye. I was unable to eat from the creatures, the offspring of those we had fed and scooped after. I knew their habits too well.

My brothers and their fledgling tribes had no concern to match mine. They built up beside the altar a roasting stone. Slaughtered gifts for The Maker and a smoked portion, lifted by the sacramental fork, for themselves.

I told Paan the rain ribbon, as she called it, looked to me more like a battle bow--without an arrow, pointing toward the heavens, away from the earth. The rain bow. A sign of peace.

      Here again, more imagined harmony drooled from my lips.

I return again to the thought with which I started. Even with so many words already fallen from my nib, I remain attracted to the ease of having not picked up the stylus to write. But I willingly take the opportunity to defend myself against how this narrative will be read--and how my firstborn bears the weight.

I will tell it again, what happened so long ago. I will tell it once more.

I will answer the questions.

For the last time.

Yes, I was going to his tent to speak with him about the next season's planting, the dividing and driving of the spring herd. I called his name. There was no answer. I called again. He gave no response.

I pulled back the hide of his tent to the odors of sweat and spilt, day-old wine. In the warm, dim light, he lay on his back, naked, asleep, his gray beard stained purple.

No, I did not cover him. A laugh rose up and bubbled out of me. Here he was, The Maker's mouthpiece. His high priest, in a heap of sweaty wrinkles and flab, his loins bare and slack in the humid afternoon air. For all he had become, in those few moments under my gaze I had power over him. He was ancient, hairy-bottomed, and helpless.

I stood over him and felt my muscle and youth. If even for a moment, I felt what it was to rule. A pair of flies buzzed past me, circled and haloed his head. I turned, his bloated and slumbering frame at my back. I stood in the open door of his tent. I looked out over the land and let the joy of the moment rise and warm me.

Shem/Visi l Japheth/Elhana l **Ham**/Paan

Yes. That evening I told Shem and Japheth.

I said to them, *listen to this*.

I laughed and said to them, *he was of no use at all*.

I said to them, *I picked up his staff. I stood in his tent and looked down at his limp and snoring form. Then I did what he could not. I turned and looked out across the land.*

But my brothers did not laugh. They stared at me. They then turned and ran to his tent and went in walking toe to heel, a cover of wool draped behind them. They covered him.

An act of honor, they said.

W

Shem/Visi I Japheth/Elhana I **Ham**/Paan

Which of them roused him from his stupor? Which of them repeated to him words meant only for them? Japheth or Shem told him how he lay under my gaze. I must scour these writings for a clue.

Wrapped in the wool with which they had covered him, sleep clogging his bloodshot eyes, his long gray hair uncombed and lifted by the dawn breeze, he passed judgment upon me by cursing my son and my son's sons.

The punishment was too great. It was more than I could bear.

I'd striven with him through the building and the leaving. The days upon nights upon days on the waters. And then this? His stinking breath forms a final prophetic vision? With a jaw full of words, he cleaves my firstborn's clan from the rest of mankind?

What was left for me? A wife with a drowned past, a shattered spirit, and a cursed son not yet weaned from her breast.

Shem/Visi I Japheth/Elhana I **Ham**/Paan

No. My anger did not cool as I stood again in his tent watching the last falls of his chest. He'd soon have the gift of being out of range while I'd be left, the gray and bitter patriarch of servant-sons.

I only ever wanted to share with him in what he had. To rule as he had ruled.

And as I look, here again, I have come and given it more words than I wished.

Paan has come and will now finish her story. Unless I miss my guess, she is no less eager to be done speaking of this past. No less desirous of leaving this place for the last time.

W

Shem/Visi I Japheth/Elhana I **Ham**/Paan

Paan, Wife of Ham

We stepped from the ramp onto the rock that formed the mountains we would come to call Ararat. I moved slowly as we began our descent into the valley. My legs were swollen. My calves and ankles had lost their boundaries. Elhana on one side, Visi on the other, the child bore down on my insides, its weight like one of the many boulders over which we were climbing.

The smell of water and lingering rot gave me such nausea. Burning, rising in my throat--yes, even as I write this the smell is stitched into my memory, if not laced into the very lining and thin hair of my nostrils. Even as I write this, I lift my hand to my face. I cup it over my nose and mouth in an unthinking attempt to defend myself against the stench that shimmered all around us.

Yes, there among the rocks of Ararat, my water spilled, and the sounds of my cries echoed.

Ithought of taking my new son to meet my mother and father, but like so many thoughts that surface before they are fully known, this one met facts and was rendered void.

W

Shem/Visi I Japheth/Elhana I Ham/**Paan**

M y first and unblessed son took his last suckle from my breast.

Unblessed is not the same as cursed.

This is what Ham says to me when I didn't speak for two moons. Then four.

It seems Ham spoke prophecy too. The difference between him and Noah is he didn't realize he was a prophet.

This is the most dangerous kind.

I've seen many rain ribbons since that one. All are mere shadows.

That one filled the sky with such color the shore, pastures, and cliffs took on its hue. We stood awash in its steamy ink.

W

Ham told me what he'd done, what he'd seen and felt in his father's tent.

I heard the word *drunken*.

I stopped him at the word *naked*.

But he continued, speaking in tones both confession and brag.

Canaan was a child. He heard his grandfather speak his name.

Once, twice, three times.

He smiled and looked up toward the tent and his grandfather's raised arms. He started to run to greet him, but after a few paces stopped.

The tone of voice settled over him. He paused, uncertain over the many words that surrounded the call of his name. He turned back toward me, his small brow creased, the question of what he'd heard about to pass from his lips.

All the tricks used to ease a child failed.

He'd heard the tone. This was enough.

There is great pain in childbirth.

And the pain endures.

Shem/Visi | Japheth/Elhana | Ham/**Paan**

Ham's ambition was attractive to me when we were young. I was the focus of his lust--of his conquest. But too soon it was always something else. Then it was always someone else.

With the Effort, Ham became obsessed with Noah and what part of Noah's greatness he might grasp for himself. He spoke day and night of carrying on the rule of Noah, of holding Noah's staff into his own old age. As he told me of gazing at his father's fallen nakedness there was a renewed delight in his eyes.

I've never said this, but I became glad for the curse.

Not for the curse--Canaan's burden is my own--but for the separation it caused. It made room for Ham and me. We gathered our few goods and left, driving our flocks ahead of us.

We sought to put behind us these dark words and the effects on our son. And we were successful, for a time. But now it is the line and labor of Canaan that is laying the foundation for Babel's tower.

They are servants to another vision.

With Noah failing, we've returned, Ham and I, for a few days to see Naamah. And to write our words here.

Seeing Elhana and Visi again, we speak of our children, our grandchildren, life since we first came to the lake shore. We don't speak of the Once Past or the Effort. Those words we've left here. We don't--we won't--pick them up again.

Shem/Visi | Japheth/Elhana | Ham/**Paan**

Naamah, Wife of Noah

Wife. Midwife. I was both.

To be a woman well along in years is to be a woman who helps bring forth life. I've seen many children born, but none born on a bed of rock partway down a mountain.

Like a ewe or jenny drawn to shelter by the pangs, Paan found a cleft and lay splayed out in its cool shade. Elhana, Visi, and I formed a wall, making a birthing hovel. Sunlight fled. With her pants of labor the air trapped against the rock grew stale and damp. Paan lay naked, propped up on a bundle of straw, her forehead shiny, her limbs shaking with fatigue.

Canaan came by moonlight, no living human sharing the day or place of his birth. I lifted him, his body hot and wet. He arched his back and released a brief, gurgling cry as I gave him to Paan. She pulled him to her breast and wept.

Sobs for more than his coming.

Our clothes filthy and torn, our minds worn thin from the wooden maze of dank and stink, we had stepped from the ramp of the Effort and squinted toward the empty horizon. We were bruised, calloused, and in desperate need of sleep. But we were alive. Our feet left prints in soil once again.

A holy exile.

With the tang of forbidden citrus in the corner of her mouth and a man by her side whom she was learning to love all over again, perhaps this was Eve's thought too as she stepped over the threshold out of Eden—as she too stepped into a barren, muted landscape, weighed down with the memories of a place she'd once called home.

We must thank The Maker for saving us, and for preserving these.

Noah gestured to the creatures scattering into the vast landscape, few of which remained to be seen.

We give thanks for the re-creation, the raising out of the void. We alone were lifted up and out of the watery expanse...a remnant...Your remnant.

His words and the wind were the only sounds—the lone priest and The Maker.

And I did give thanks. My sons had all been saved and their wives with them and now we had a son's son. No other mother had lived to see such gratitudes. So I offered up—on behalf of all women—a thanksgiving. For life after loss.

Yet, the questions pulled at me again and again, like a beggar's tug at my cloak. Could not more have been rescued? Could not more have believed?

I reminded myself, these questions were answered by a simple fact—there we nine stood.

On the shore of the lake we gathered in the morning light. The water, reflecting the blue of the sky above, lapped against its rim of pebbles and litter. We uttered once more our dreams of pulling down handfuls of firm fruit and filling jugs with oil. We then passed between us the now dry and brittle sprig the dove had retrieved. We knew well the leaf of the olive tree, its long thin structure of ribs, its smooth skin and soft hue. Even so, we studied it, each of us holding it between the tips of our fingers.

And we began that moment to search for another leaf like it, newly unfurled from even a single shoot.

In the sawdust alongside the tools I had packed all we needed for cooking, weaving, and making wax lamps. I gathered the women together, those from whom all future mankind would come, and we began.

We could have changed—made new ways, carved new routines in our days. But we were eager to find ourselves once again—to make and reclaim the familiar.

The gift of a new start is so rare it is often missed, overlooked, and squandered. We are quick to grasp, instead, what we know, to return to those shapes that fit us.

After the withheld blessing, Paan and I gave the child a warm bath. He floated naked in the water, an unknowing smile creasing his lips.

I did not hide my thoughts from Paan.

This husband of mine—must we now find meaning in his silence as well as his words? Has he become a seer for whom even the absence of language holds meaning?

Paan looked up at me. She touched my arm and looked me in the eye.

Thank you, she said.

But words would come.

Noah would fill his silence. Overflow and blot it out.

Noah spoke the prophecy over Canaan.

Before nightfall, Paan began preparations to leave.

Women are pulled into the messes men make and tasked with forming structure of them.

I saw Ham's face at Noah's words. How can a woman endure the opposing souls of the son of her womb and the man of her youth?

w

As the years pass, too frequent is the visitation of the twins regret and anger—regret when we have caused our own pain, anger when another has.

Their icy messages feel alike in the night.

I am the widow of Noah, the once unknown survivor, his most intimate companion.

I was his accomplice and partner in that decreed de-creation; his lover, confidant, and critic through all that came after.

The marks I've placed here give only shades of the story. They are like snippets of whisper overheard in the dark.

Noah/**Naamah**

Last Words

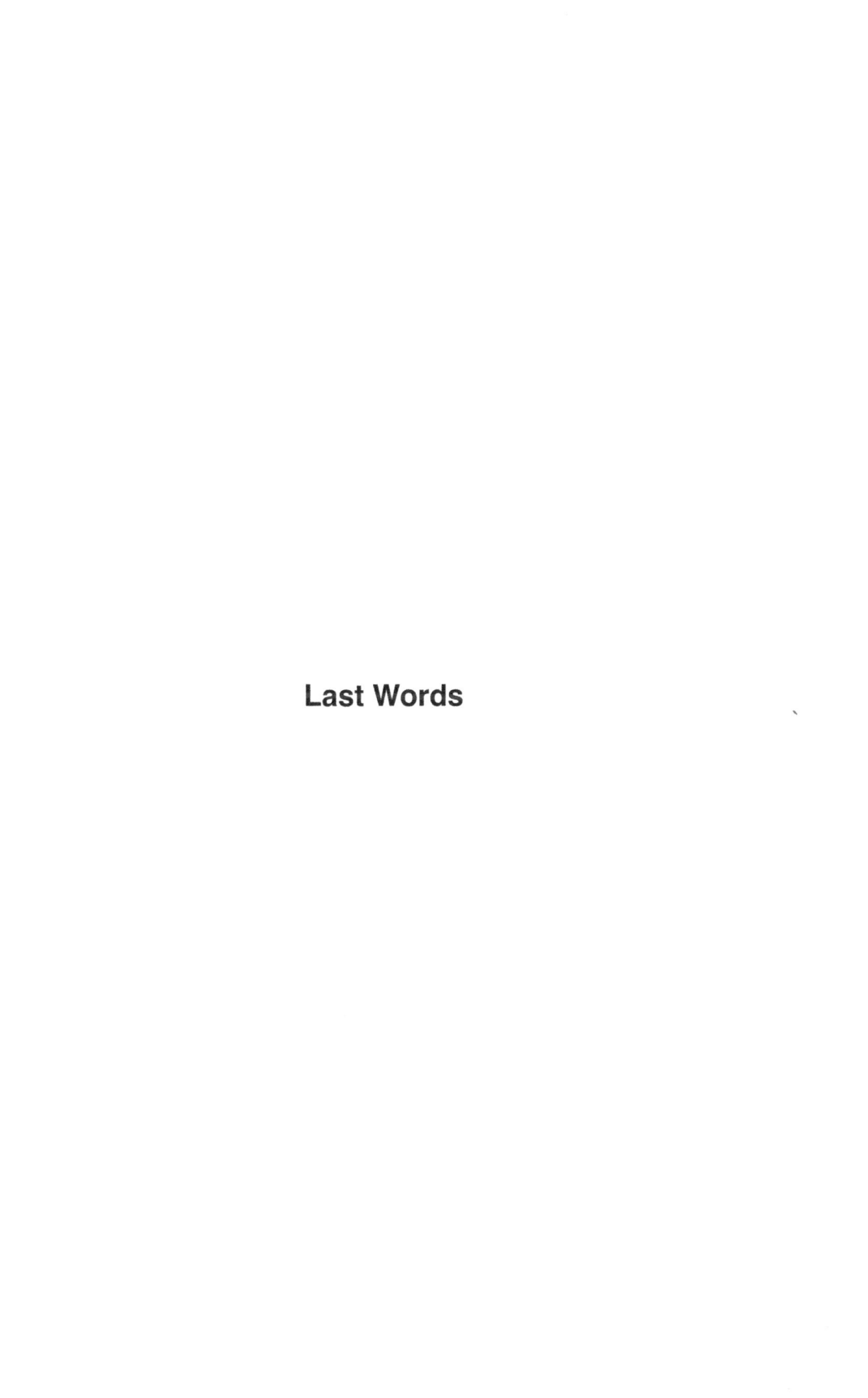

Dedan of Babel

W

Before we shear them, we lift, wade in, and wash our sheep in the waters--in the lake that remains from the flood.

It is true.

Those waters bring fertility and take away disease. I have seen it in my own flock!

Kittim of Etrucsia

I am a descendant of the clan of Japheth. I am a designer and builder by trade. In the last few years, I have seen a curious movement. There is a great deal of demand for gopher wood from the ark. Gopher can be found nowhere else. The wealthiest herdsmen and those with a stake in the lake trade are requesting planks be harvested from the ark of Noah and be used to adorn their homes.

The ark is slowly being whittled away. In my children's children's lifetimes it will be gone.

Eva of Shinar

I am barren. Six bloody knots are my husband's heirs. What use am I?

Our elder, Shem, is the last remaining of the first family. He is delighted by each birth and blesses each child born.

I yearn to hear his blessing over a child of mine. In the shade of his olive grove, his calloused and bony hand under each child's thigh, his ancient accent thick with meaning.

Swarm, he says, *swarm*.

Obal of Mesha

A man killed another in the night. The Law of Noah requires he die. This time it was enforced. The man was taken up, bound hand and foot, and thrown from the eastern cliff of Ararat. The vultures scattered as he landed on the pile of weathered bones at its base.

Murders are not as uncommon as you might think. Those of means find their way around the threat of such punishment. And in some settlements Noah's law holds more authority than in others. In any case, being caught is by far the greater error.

Leah of Nippur

I am Leah. I am from the lineage of Canaan. I am named after a dear friend of my great grandmother Naamah.

My name and life are a constant reminder of those that did not make the voyage on Noah's floating vessel of salvation.

Can life be easy for one whose namesake was a lost soul? Can one rise above a memory not one's own, but inherited? Bequeathed at birth?

I for one cannot.

Riphath of Tartesso

There is a colony that still seeks after the God of Noah. They keep ancient and naive ways, proving harmless in their backward devotion. Smoke rises from their sacrifices. Sweet aroma to their Maker hangs like fog over the northern corner of Babel.

They repeat strange hymns in unison.

> *While the earth remains,*
> *sowing and harvest,*
> *summer and winter*
> *sunlight and moonlight will not cease.*

And when a rainbow appears, they stare into the clouds and fall speechless.

To us their practice of faith is foolishness, but to those who believe it is said to be the power of God.

Uzal of Sephar

This morning I traveled to one of the villages at the base of the mountains. There, still visible under the brush and briars, I walked on the first road made of timbers, laid in soft earth by our ancestors as they came off the ark.

I then climbed up, over the rocks, and stood in the shadow of the ancient hull. I rested my back against its hand-hewn edge. And as I looked up, a dove circled then landed on the highest remaining perch. Its coo filled the canyon.

Sabtah of Accad

The past is in the memories of the old, but more so in our soil.

A man I know is opening a house along the lakefront where he will display items that have been unearthed while digging wells and making roads in and out of Babel. Many of these items are said to be from before the flood.

I was not sure what this meant—the flood. I had been told there was a flood that covered the entire earth. Such truth tasked the imagination. It begged for a story.

And here that story has been told.

Notes on the Text

The section epigraphs, the quote of Genesis 5.29 (Lemech's blessing at Noah's birth), the quote of Genesis 1.2, and the quotes from Genesis 9 (the laws) are from Robert Alter's translation of Genesis as found in *The Five Books of Moses*.

The following line was borrowed from my debut novel, *The Confessions of Adam*. "... He'd hung them with care in the spot He'd prepared for them, while others He joyfully flung into the void, arcs of fiery white light streaming as they crossed over and passed each other."

The insight on the timing of Methuselah's death was gained and the meaning of his name was quoted from Jeff Kinley's book, *As it Was in the Days of Noah*.

The following lines are quoted from Frederick Buechner's "A Sprig of Hope" from his book *Secrets in the Dark: A Life in Sermons*.

> And as the waters rose, so rose the sounds of battle for the few remaining pieces of dry ground. Perhaps the chaos was no greater than it had ever been. Only wetter.

> ... in a wilderness of waves.

His eyes closed, his lashes watery wet, his cheek touched the dove's breast. Could he feel the tiny panic of her heart?

The phrase "Unless I miss my guess" was a favorite of Buechner's, appearing often in *Secrets in the Dark*.

The paraphrases of Genesis 7 (the command to take pairs of animals), Genesis 8-9 (God's covenant), Genesis 9 (the judgment on Canaan), Ecclesiastes 5.2, John 1.5, and 1 Corinthians 1.18 are my own, from the English.

The idea of the rainbow as a battle bow is from Bruce Waltke's landmark commentary, *Genesis*.

Cræft by Alexander Langlands, though not quoted, fed my imagination as I sought to conceive how work was accomplished in ancient times.

One entry was written by my wife, Cyndi, who has come to know my written voice so well. We leave it to the reader to guess which.

Acknowledgments and Gratitudes

In coming to be, each novel takes its own unpredictable and meandering path.
This one certainly did.

Thank you to the members of Westside Writers Workshop. It was during a writing exercise with you, on 10 March 2018, I wrote the first lines of what would become a manuscript on this narrative and ultimately *Waterborne*. You are my writing community.

In early 2020 my late friend, Steve Burgan, took me and a group of other colleagues through his Full-Spectrum Thinking (FuST) process, a brainstorming and decision-making workshop. Through this exercise I chose this project over several others. My friend, a participant in the marketplace of ideas, lost to cancer May 2022. Thank you, Steve. I can't drive past McAllister's without thinking of you.

Thank you to the thoughtful readers who provided invaluable feedback at each juncture of this project as it grew more and more unwieldy before finally being (somewhat) tamed.

> Thank you to my 2020 beta readers - Warren and Tillie Burns, Alan Clingan, Pat & Melissa Denton, Jim & Amy Knapp, Michelle Lamb, and Rita Gerard-O'Riley.

Thank you to my 2021 beta readers - Sharon Cromer's Ladies Bible Study, The Divine Scouts. Diana Paige, Laura Crosby, Rhonda Rosenbaum, Sharon Cromer, Vanda Terrell, and Shirley Moss. This was the first time I'd done a beta reading group. It won't be the last!

And thank you to my 2022 beta readers - Darrell and Wendi Campbell.

Thank you to my daughter, Julia Peterson, who has graciously joined my creative team, directing social media, and letting me focus on the work of making story.

Thank you to Dr. Brent Krammes and Dr. Lauren Rich as well as the Department of Humanities and the School of Arts and Sciences at Grace College for welcoming me back to campus for the 2022 Fall B session to teach Intermediate Fiction writing—while working on the final draft of this manuscript. This gift resulted in two energizing classes a week for eight weeks with seven fellow writers: Abby, Reagan, Heidi, Beverly, Mackenzie, Joey, and Riley. Thank you for all the conversation about what makes good writing great!

Thank you to Karen Sargent and all of you on the *Waterborne* Launch Team! Your excitement and dedication were a sight to behold. Keep the lines open. I'm writing the next novel.

Thank you to my agent, Joëlle Delbourgo, who continues to believe in and support my writing. I continue to be grateful to Ben H. Winters for introducing us.

Thank you to George and Karen Porter, as well as the entire team at Bold Vision Books, for enthusiastically investing and reinvesting in my creative efforts.

My gratitude to Cynthia Ruchti for her careful <u>and</u> encouraging edit of this manuscript.

And at last to my wife, Cyndi, who remains by my side, enjoying the ups and suffering the downs of this writerly life. She tells me when the writing is working--and more importantly, when it isn't. I don't write without her.

MEET DAVID J. MARSH

Dave grew up steeped in biblical narratives. His mom read to him. His dad was a pastor, a student of theology and biblical languages. Dave often asked his dad to read aloud the scriptures in their original Hebrew and Greek. While Dave could not understand them, the music of these languages fascinated him.

In his 2021 Illumination Award medalist and 2020 Oregon Christian Writers Cascade Award finalist debut novel, *The Confessions of Adam* (Bold Vision Books, 2019), a re-telling of the universal and dramatic narrative that opens the book of Genesis, he has crafted a richly imagined story of the creation and its aftermath. Dave is also the author of *A Conversation on Genesis 2-4: Study Guide* (Bold Vision Books, 2020).

Dave holds a BS in Communications from Grace College and an MFA in Creative Writing (Fiction) from Butler University. Dave has taught at Grace College, facilitates the Westside Writers Workshop, and every other Wednesday, he posts a column on the craft of fiction called "Revel and Rant" at www.davidjmarsh.com.

A native of Indiana, Dave lives in Avon, with his wife Cyndi.

Please join Dave on Instagram and Facebook @ davidjmarshauthor, and on Twitter @marshjdavid. Email him at dave@davidjmarsh.com.

Learn more about Dave and his work at www.davidjmarsh.com.